LOVESICK LAKE

A Darkish Romantic Farce

Allison McWood

Annelid Press

This book is a work of fiction. The characters, incidents and dialogue are drawn from the author's imagination and are not to be construed as real. Any resemblance to actual events or persons, living or dead, is entirely coincidental.

FIRST EDITION

Cover design and by: Graham Kennedy

ISBN: 978-1-990292-06-4

CHAPTER ONE

Lydia Knapp blinked.

Somehow this was not how she imagined it. Poised with a silver sharpie alongside a pile of crisp, unopened novels, Lydia took a deep breath. The bookstore manager, she was sure, was peering around a bookshelf, giving her an embittered glare. She could not actually see him doing this, but she could feel his capricious eyes boring into her like a screwdriver.

She looked around the hollow store, which was peppered with an insignificant number of browsers, leafing through books and mindlessly shoving them back, askew on the shelves. She winced as a boringly average man who she secretly named Gord, bent the cover of a perfectly enjoyable William Faulkner book in his haste.

People's disrespect for literature was maddening.

Maybe if she focused on the glass entrance doors ahead of her book signing table, Lydia could telepathically conjure some readers to gather for autographs. She had hoped the turnout would be better than this. Obviously, with her book being launched by a local micro-publisher who only publishes one book every two years, she was not expecting to be staving fans off with a cattle prod. But she was hoping for at least a dozen or so. Just enough to spare her the embarrassment of being banished forever from this or any other bookstore. Because bookstores exchange gossip about unlucrative indie writers, don't they?

Phlegm of annoyance was cleared from the throat of the store manager who was hovering behind Lydia like a creepy shadow. A sanctimonious shadow. Lydia nearly gave herself whiplash as she jerked her head nearly all the way around to see the judgmental specter looming above. Clearly, Lydia forgot that she was not an owl. And the kink in her neck would remind her of this mistake for three to five days.

"Is your thing finished?" the manager asked, jerking his head towards Lydia's pathetic little drift of novels, primly piled with geometric perfection.

"Thing?" Lydia asked quizzically.

"We need this table for the Margaret Atwood display," the manager yawned as he surveyed the swelling crowd of Lydia Knapp fans who did not exist, elbowing their way through the store in pursuit of autographs. Or not.

"Well... see," Lydia stammered.

"I'm fond of Margaret Atwood," the manager said, squinting.

"As am I," Lydia garbled, nervously adjusting her slouchy hat with the ginormous, silk peony blossom. Despite her periodic bouts of social anxiety, Lydia always knew exactly how to wear a hat.

"She was my childhood crush, in fact," the manager said unromantically while crossing his arms.

"Good for you," Lydia swallowed. "Margaret Atwood is indeed a national treasure. It's just that I..."

"You're needlessly occupying a table."

"I'm booked until noon actually..."

"Aren't you embarrassed just sitting here like a schmo?"

"It's my first novel."

"No kidding," the manager said, dimpling into a smirk that made Lydia wither into her seat.

"Excuse me," Lydia said with shallow breaths, quickly pulling out her cell phone. "I need to text my publisher."

"Pussywillow Press?" the manager spat with a farty laugh. "Nobody has ever heard of them. I asked around."

Lydia frantically texted her husband, blinking some stinging tears that were rapidly reddening her eyes.

"Hunter, help!"

Lydia drummed her fingers anxiously on the table for seven full seconds before her phone buzzed with a reply.

"In a meeting. What's up, Lyds?"

"At the bookstore. Where are you?"

"Read above text."

"Please come. PLEASE."

"Can't. Sorry, Babe."

"But nobody showed up. Like at all."

"I'll make it up to you. Promise."

"Smug manager is hovering. Please."

"Can't. Bye."

"But they'll make me surrender my table in a minute."

No reply.

"This is humiliating."

No reply.

"Hunter?"

No reply.

The blood instantly rushed to Lydia's face as she heard the store manager click his tongue condescendingly. But a nanosecond later, Lydia experienced a minor electrical shock in her ribcage as the glass doors in front of her dinged and opened, revealing the eager, pimpled face of a gangly teenager. His eyes zeroed in on Lydia as he ran his fingers through his tangled shock of hair in a futile attempt to look presentable.

Lydia's jaw dropped as the knobby-elbowed youth approached her. As though he actually knew who she was. She gaped stupidly when she saw her book in the teenager's hand, dogeared and tattered with copious post-it notes sticking out every which way.

"Ms. Knapp?" the teenager squeaked unintentionally.

Lydia nodded, feeling like her head was suddenly filled with a kind of dreamy cotton.

"I can't believe it's you!" the teenager said in a jittery way while nervously thumbing through scads of pages with way too many highlighted passages.

"It's me," Lydia said with a bewildered hiccup.

The store manager quirked an eyebrow and walked away, gesturing to Lydia that he would be keeping an eye on things.

Before the teenager had a chance to lose his nerve he blurted out, "I love Mildew."

"Excuse me?" Lydia said, wondering if all fans were this unhinged or if this guy was just special.

"Sorry," the teenager said, shaking the embarrassment from his head. "Logan. Me. I'm Logan. And you're Lydia Knapp. Holy Jeez. Sorry, it's just... I have your picture taped inside my locker. Anyhow. Mildew. My absolute favorite. The character. Not the fungal hyphae in case that wasn't clear. Mr. Mildew. In this here book."

Suddenly bursting through the doors, three vivid figures approached the table and waited in line behind babbling Logan. Lydia gleamed with familiarity. Meredith, Patrice and Jules had decided to make an appearance after all. And what better timing with this doting, literary spaniel ahead of them in line. This was sure to impress her friends.

"Thank you... Logan, is it?"

Logan nodded his head so fervently, it nearly detached from his neck and flung across the room.

"I appreciate your enthusiasm," Lydia continued primly, while giving her friends a nod of acknowledgment.

"I'm totally obsessed with Mildew," Logan chattered on like a fool. "Like the significance surrounding his character."

Lydia cocked her head.

"How he's an elaborate metaphor," Logan continued, intently pointing at a highlighted passage in the well-worn pages, "of the baseness of society."

Meredith and Patrice each raised an impressed, penciled-on eyebrow at each other.

Lydia, on the other hand, looked utterly perplexed.

"And then there's the profound symbolism of his car," Logan nodded eagerly, smiling with more teeth than an overzealous crocodile.

"His car?" Lydia asked, nestling her chin on her hands in amusement and intrigue.

"He drives a Pinto!" Logan said with epiphany. "Brilliant! Pinto. Horse. Trojan. War. War can be traced back to society. It's all society's fault!"

The misinterpretation of the novel was adorable, and Lydia resisted the urge to laugh. She was reveling in the fact that her trio of female cobbers were lapping up the glamor of having her writing analyzed. By a person she was not related to no less. So what if her fan was like what, in the eleventh grade?

"And I love," Logan continued, wringing his hands together, "how you hid the concept of rejection behind the quirky persona of Catherine. So relevant in terms of society rejecting us all."

After biting her cheek contemplatively for a moment, Lydia decided against sparing the poor lad any further embarrassment. She saw this as an opportunity to look lofty in front of Meredith, Patrice and Jules. Lydia had no idea why she felt the need to impress them so badly. It's not like she had any biting desire to fit into any kind of clique. But somehow the opinion of these three meant something to her. They had known each other since high school, after all.

"Really," Lydia said to Logan with a twinge of irony in her tone. "I was under the impression that people reject *society*."

Logan's mouth moved around, looking for words. Clearly, he was not prepared for Lydia's response.

"I..." Logan stammered. "I wrote a five-paragraph essay for my Canadian I it class. Mr. Tuft said..."

"Society's big, kid," Lydia said in a way that she perceived as intellectual. "What aspect of it do you hate?"

In a state of faux shock (and perhaps pride) of Lydia's bold retort, the glossy red lips of Meredith, Patrice and Jules simultaneously formed into identical letter O's. Did they share the same wand of *Sassy Pomegranate* lipstick? If so, that would be unhygienic. But they did look glamorously uniform which was clearly their intention.

The lower lip of Logan quivered briefly before he enthusiastically changed the subject.

"I'm a writer too!" Logan quipped. "Like you! Er... Not like you specifically. Because you're famous and basically perfect. I'm in Grade Eleven so..."

"Good for you," Lydia said cordially as she signed his book. She bit her lip in a conscious effort not to giggle at the irony of this young twerp thinking she was famous.

"Also, I'd like to purchase another copy, please. For my uncle."

"Your uncle is a fan of chick lit, is he?"

"Books are kind of his thing," Logan said earnestly. "All kinds of books. He doesn't care so much about genre as he does quality. His name is Floyd."

"Give Uncle Floyd my regards," Lydia said cordially.

"I can introduce you if you want," Logan said eagerly. "I think he would really dig you."

"That's okay," Lydia politely declined, dreading the thought of being set up with somebody's girly book-loving Uncle Floyd.

"But you're totally his type!" Logan insisted. "He's been looking for someone like you for a long time! You're literally perfect for him. And believe me, he's a man who knows what he wants."

"Flattered," Lydia said with swelling revulsion, "but uninterested. Thank you though."

Logan deflated with disappointment but quickly recharged with another sudden wave of enthusiasm.

"May I ask," Logan squeaked adolescently, "how do you get inside people's heads the way you do? What inspired Mr. Mildew?"

Closing the signed book, Lydia replied, "My uncle. He drove a Pinto."

Logan nodded with his eager smile, trying in his mind to find the profundity in what Lydia said. He walked away absentmindedly, admiring the signature in his favorite book.

"Lydia Knapp," Patrice said, smacking her lips in that special, attention-seeking way she had. "*Our* Lydia Knapp."

"Was that a *fan* just now?" Meredith said, gesturing with a hand flourish. "You have a fan. Girls, she has fans."

"Did I do okay?" Lydia asked, suddenly self-conscious. "I'm kind of new to this whole *commiserating with the public* thing."

"You're perfect," Patrice said, giving Lydia a lip-glossed kissy pucker in the air. Was this gesture pretentious? Or adorable? You decide.

"You did it, Lyds!" said Jules while sipping a smoothie of a greenish hue. "We always knew you'd be famous."

Famous. There was that word again. Pussywillow Press was hardly a launch pad into the world of infinite wealth and fame of Kardashian proportions. The irony of this misunderstanding wiggled around in her gut, but she decided not to correct them.

"Sign these," Patrice said, plopping two copies of the novel in front of Lydia.

"Two copies?"

"One's for Biscotti," Patrice said, unzipping her purse and revealing a hamster-sized teacup poodle dressed in human baby clothing.

"Patrice," Lydia warned, "put that thing away. You can't bring a dog in the store."

"I don't talk about your babies that way," Patrice pouted with her weirdly cushiony lips.

"I don't have babies," Lydia replied curtly.

"Well, that isn't any of my business, is it," Patrice said indignantly. "Go ahead. Sign. Captial B. Small i..."

"The dog can't read, Patrice," Meredith said dryly with a superior eyeball roll.

"He's gifted," Patrice said in baby talk that was embarrassing to everyone in the room except Patrice. "Aren't you, Biscotti? *Aren't you?*"

"Okay, *that's* not burgeoning on psychotic," Meredith said sardonically. "What time are you off, Lyds? We're lunching."

"I actually don't have a lot of time," Lydia apologized. "I only took the morning off work so..."

"Screw work," Meredith said, raising a meticulously manicured hand.

Lydia pursed her lips as she looked at her own hand with its naked, chipped fingernails and skin that was chafing from hand sanitizer.

"Come on, Lyds," Jules coaxed. "You don't need that brain-numbing job anymore. You are a published author now."

"You, us, *The Refined Cucumber,*" Meredith said authoritatively. "I made reservations."

"Is that what you're wearing?" Patrice asked without meaning to sound pompous. She received a sharp elbow jab from Meredith.

Lydia compared her vintage, patchwork jacket to the sleek, designer garb of her friends. Meredith, for example, was dressed to the nines in her elegant power suit with its intimidating pinstripes. Patrice looked like she just fell off a Fashion Week runway. She looked like the world's sexiest sausage, encased tightly with name-brand silk and lace - and stiletto heels that could plausibly be weaponized if the occasion arose. Finally, Jules was on point with every latest trend. This week she sported a genuine, Icelandic sheepskin vest over a full-bodied, black bodysuit, accessorized by a pair of thigh-high prostitute boots. Or at least that was how Lydia referred to them in the privacy of her imagination.

How in the world did Lydia get accepted into this gaggle of worldly alpha-females? She was not sure how she fit in with them, but she was grateful to be included.

"Our usual table then?" Meredith said, having decided that she had already persuaded Lydia to ditch work. "We need to celebrate you, Love. And this momentous achievement of yours. Besides, I'm literally *dying* to talk to you about donating some copies of your delicious book to the silent auction at my gallery fundraiser. When that cute curator hears that my best friend wrote it…"

"Hey!" Patrice pouted again with her ridiculous lower lip.

Conflicted, Lydia checked the time on her phone and bit her lip contemplatively.

CHAPTER TWO

The Refined Cucumber reminded Lydia of a Gatsby garden party. It was a demure, little bistro with intricately uncomfortable wrought iron chairs, pristine tablecloths and doilies. Yes, doilies. Lydia was afraid to use the napkins, lest she blemish one with her lipstick or a smear of dijonnaise. Lydia cocked her head at the unusual centerpiece in the middle of the table, consisting of a glass orb containing a live butterfly. She wriggled in her seat, trying not to feel too out of place.

Lydia was startled out of her stupor when Meredith abruptly lifted a glass in a predictable toast.

"Friends!" Meredith projected with the finesse of a conscientious drama student. "To Lydia, whose success, I am sure, has made our little circle of friends all that more sophisticated."

Lydia coughed on an aptly timed crumb of shrimp cocktail.

"Cheers," said Jules, lifting a glass of something conspicuously green.

"Guys, really," Lydia said, flushing.

"How should we celebrate?" Patrice said, clasping her hands together in anticipation. "Shopping maybe?"

"I thought lunch was the celebration," Lydia said, quirking an eyebrow.

"What about that trendy, new club?" Jules asked with a ridiculous, green moustache from her mystery beverage. "They play live Icelandic music."

"Girl, what is that thing on your upper lip?" Patrice asked in utter disgust.

"Seaweed smoothie," Jules replied, discreetly licking what looked like pond scum from her face.

"Jules, that smoothie smells like sin. Avarice, I think."

"Don't make fun of my smoothie. The seaweed was extracted from the Galapagos Islands."

"That's... trendy."

"It's green," Patrice pointed out. "And it's making me curdle."

"Lyds," Meredith said confidentially. "Don't look now, but that trendy looking waiter over there is checking you out."

Lydia discreetly eyeballed a bookish waiter approaching with the bill and a flirty smirk. He was wearing a bookish turtleneck and John Lennon glasses.

"I said don't look," Meredith hissed through her teeth.

"A literary type," squealed Patrice. "Go for it, Lyds."

"Patrice, I'm married."

"Shameless flirting never hurt anyone," Patrice shrugged innocently. "Just make a coy gesture and then ignore him."

"See," Lydia audibly sighed. "This is how I landed myself a husband. By taking advice from the terminally single."

Their girlish chatter was interrupted by the plunk of the bill being set on the table. Above them hovered the shadow of an oddly fragrant waiter who went by the name of Anatole. He smelled like lychee fruit. But in a masculine way. Meredith pushed the bill in front of Lydia.

"She's a celebrity," Meredith said, gesturing towards Lydia. "Renowned author."

"You don't say," said Anatole in an indecipherable accent, taking a step back to admire the impressiveness of Lydia.

"You're exaggerating," Lydia said, withering into her chair.

"Written anything I might have read?" Anatole inquired.

"He *reads!*" Patrice excitedly stage whispered to Lydia.

Lydia shooed Patrice away.

"Probably n…" Lydia tried.

"*Fairweather Friends Forever,*" Meredith interrupted, showcasing her friend's book proudly. "We just came from her launch."

"This is a launch lunch," Patrice twittered girlishly. "Hehe I'm so funny."

Lydia kicked Patrice under the table.

"She is a very big deal," Meredith bragged.

"Mer!" Lydia hissed.

Before Lydia could stop it from happening, Anatole swiped Lydia's credit card from the table and read it aloud. "Lydia Knapp," he said thoughtfully. "Pretty. And memorable. Sounds like a name that belongs in print." And he finished with a wink that made a bat flap madly around inside Lydia's ribcage.

"The thing is though," Lydia quickly interjected while feeling for her ring finger... Oh for the love of... Lydia forgot that she sent her wedding ring in to be resized when she accidentally lost ten pounds. Stuff happens when you're too poor to eat three squares most days.

"Before you process the payment," Patrice interrupted obliviously, "can I throw an extra croissant on the tab?" Unzipping her purse, Patrice instantly began speaking in a ridiculous, cartoon voice. "You're a hungry boy, aren't you?" she said to her microscopic fur baby.

"Miss," Anatole warned, "I'm afraid there are no animals permitted here. Fur dander and all that. It's a hygiene thing."

Patrice assumed a cartoonishly offended visage.

"I don't think you want to go there," Lydia said ironically. "Patrice has delusions of giving birth to that poodle."

Anatole's eyes slowly widened like a pair of increasingly timorous golf balls. "Why don't I just get you that pastry," he said in an abrupt attempt to change the subject. "Excuse me."

As the fragrant waiter wafted away like a refreshing zephyr, Lydia noticed that he discreetly left behind a napkin upon which he wrote his name and phone number. She felt her face instantly redden. But before she had a chance to crumple the napkin and squish it in the pocket of her funky, vintage jacket, Meredith swiped the napkin and cooed like a meddlesome pigeon. Lydia withered like a humiliated geranium.

"No," Lydia said preemptively.

"Didn't I tell you the dishy waiter was vibing with you?"

"His pupils were dilated," Patrice said enthusiastically. "I was paying attention."

"What is wrong with you people?" Lydia said, shielding the flush of her face with a limp hand. "I am not interested in…"

"Then why did your face turn into a baboon's duff?"

"Do you really think I have it in me to cheat on Hunter?" Lydia said with a tightly clenched jaw. "Do you think I'm that kind of a person?"

"Who said anything about cheating?" Meredith guffawed. "Flirting never hurt anyone."

"You should call him," Patrice japed. "Just for fun."

"This whole conversation is completely disrespectful to Hunter," Lydia hissed. "I have a sweet man waiting for me at home. A sweet, *hot* man, no less. Beguiling even. Hard-working. Zestfully romantic, not that it's any of your business…"

"Loosen up, Lyds," Jules said, still nursing her smoothie. "Jeez."

"I think it's cute," Patrice piped up, "how she's defending her boo. Besides, if Lydia doesn't want him, I might be interested. I don't usually go for the intellectual type, but he smells like guava nectar and I find that alluring."

"Lychee fruit," Lydia mumbled.

Three identical expressions of mischievousness challenged Lydia from around the table.

"Give me a break," Lydia said, rolling her eyes. "Anyone with a nose can identify Anatole's aroma. "It doesn't mean I'm interested in him."

"Baboon's duff."

"Stop."

"Lydia, you can't help it if your biorhythms are compatible with another guy," Jules offered. "You're a mammal."

"Finding someone attractive is not the same as..."

"So you admit you're attracted..."

"This is literally the worst advice I've ever..."

"We're teasing," Meredith said, rolling her eyes. "We are fully aware that you are fiercely loyal to Hunter. Me? I could never imagine myself stapled to the same man for eternity. Or you know. A month and a half."

"Respect," Jules said, forming a peace sign with two fingers.

"Love is so cute," Patrice said, accidentally speaking in baby talk again.

Lydia took a deep breath. She was really not all that good with confrontation of any kind. She loathed how her social anxiety would creep out of its gopher hole whenever people around her got too intense or ganged up on her. She secretly prayed to the gods of normalcy that she did not freak out her three best friends and dreaded the idea of them giggling about her at the fingernail salon or the elite sauna of gossip. Or worse, would they lose their patience with Lydia's periodic loss of social graces and ditch her completely? Who would she have lunch with? Who else would tolerate her quirks?

While collecting herself, Lydia indulged in a momentary mediation on *all things Hunter.* He was the one consistent, unwavering thing in her life. A stabilizing presence. No matter how weird she got. Regardless of how her brain conspicuously worked differently than the brains of others. Regardless of her unorthodox career choice. Hunter would always be there for her. She had zero interest in turning her head in the direction of any other man. Hunter was *her person.*

"Frig!" Lydia said a little more shrilly than she intended when she suddenly noticed the time. "My lunch hour is over. I need to go," she said, scrambling for her things. "Like now."

"Why are you still working at that horrible job?" Meredith asked.

"People who are interested in money and respect generally don't become writers," Lydia said in a feeble attempt at channeling her current feeling of awkwardness into humor. "In other news, I need to buy groceries occasionally. As well as other things that keep me alive."

"But you're famous now," Patrice reminded her.

Pretending not to hear Patrice's incorrect statement, Lydia scrambled from the table and fumbled out of *Refined Cucumber*.

"You know what she needs?" Meredith said ponderingly.

"A chiffon cocktail dress," Patrice nodded definitively.

"What for?" Meredith chuffed. "When does she ever go out anywhere? All she does is write and work. What she needs is... well, *us.*"

CHAPTER THREE

Braving the hectic Toronto traffic, Lydia mounted her bicycle and ventured into the honking, fumy nightmare. Living in the city was Lydia's own personal hell. Pandemonium of *John Milton proportions*. The bustle of people made her ill at ease. Everyone just disconnectedly milling around, averting eye contact like a society of lobotomized clones. How could anyone feel so isolated in a city so bursting at the seams with humans?

Passing the clock tower at the Old City Hall, Lydia swallowed a ball of anxiety when she realized just how late she was.

***

Hostility has a distinct smell. And Lydia was overwhelmed by this odor the moment she set foot into her stagnant office. Diane Ubervich, Lydia's emotionally deceased boss, was standing at the door like a starched shirt, waiting for Lydia to arrive. Her metallic eyes were windowed by a pair of severe, horn-rimmed glasses, boring into Lydia's soul.

"How nice of you to join us," Ubervich said with a voice that sliced through Lydia's self-esteem like butter. "And only four and a half hours late."

"Sixteen minutes actually," Lydia said, barely audible as she averted eye contact on her way to her boring cubicle.

"Really," Ubervich said with an inflection that was clearly not interrogative. By now she was crossing her arms like a disciplinary pedagogue.

"I was at my signing…"

"Mmmhmmm."

"Then I took my lunch break…"

"Of course," Ubervich interrupted obliviously, "it wouldn't occur to one to let one know when one is going to saunter into the office at whatever hour pleases one."

"I booked the morning off."

"I hired you against my better judgment," Ubervich snarled, "and the fervent warnings of my superiors. I was told artists are liabilities. Off in their own little worlds. Noncommital. Off-balance. Damaged. Delusional."

"I brought you a copy of my book."

"But I hired you anyway," Ubervich said, clearly not paying attention to Lydia. "And do you know why? Because I am a deeply compassionate individual."

"Maybe I should just…"

As Lydia finally made it to her desk, Ubervich suddenly discovered that she had Lydia's book in her hand.

"What in the world is this?" Ubervich said, holding the book limply in her fingers as though she accidentally picked up a live eel.

"I thought you might like…"

"Is this a gift?"

"I…"

"I don't believe this," Ubervich said, reviled. "It's completely inappropriate."

"Where are you going?" Lydia asked her boss who was now trotting out of the room.

"Lodging a formal complaint," Ubervich said over her shoulder. "This sort of behavior cannot be tolerated."

"What?"

"Offering gifts to one's superiors is strictly forbidden by company policy."

"Just give it back then," Lydia twitched. "Jeez."

"Consider this duly noted," Ubervich seethed, pointing a meticulously manicured finger in Lydia's general direction. "One more crafty maneuver like this… Two words. Out. Source."

"That's one word actually."

***

When Lydia returned to her desk, she discovered a pile of backlogged paperwork awaiting her. This data entry job bored her to sobs. She was much too educated for this kind of soul-sucking torture. And her work environment was even less inspiring than the inside of a styrofoam cup. The office was sterile, stark and asylum-like.

Nobody seemed to notice that Lydia was not in the office that morning. Everyone was just blandly milling about like a factory of automatons. There in the sea of soulless clerks, individuality and other such frivolities did not matter. Lydia just stood there stupidly with her book in hand, watching her dreary fate walk around in front of her.

The sheer volume of paper on her desk made her deflate.

So. Much. Paper.

Her swivel chair screeched as Lydia sat down. She squinted in a headachy way from the flickering, fluorescent lights. Her fingers began to clack monotonously on her keyboard as she transcribed a plethora of contextless numbers. Again. While mindlessly clacking her keyboard with one hand, she used the other to secretly pull out a notebook. Occasionally, she would jot down random thoughts, so long as nobody was watching.

An intense coworker rubbernecked around the adjacent cubicle and stared at Lydia with bulging eyes while she scrawled hastily in her notebook. She felt his eyes on her and momentarily stopped writing, at which point, Rubberneck quickly pulled his head back behind his cubicle. A nanosecond later he prairie dogged above his cubicle and stared at her with laser focus.

"Hi, Creepy-Guy-In-the-Cubicle-Next-to-Mine," Lydia said blandly.

Rubberneck startled for a moment before replying in his token, intense manner with wide, penetrating eyes.

"What are you writing?" Rubberneck asked a little too intensely.

"Nothing," Lydia lied, still writing.

"I see you writing," Rubberneck said with a neurotic quaver. "You have a notebook and you're writing in it. You can't do that you know."

"Why don't you crawl back into your cubicle and play with your spiders?"

"I know who you are," Rubberneck said. "You don't think I do, but I do."

"Who am I, Rubberneck?"

"You shouldn't be here," Rubberneck continued with his eyes bulging even more spherically if that was even possible. "You're famous. Famous people shouldn't be working in a place like this. They watch us here."

"Not famous, Rubberneck."

"You are though."

"You are mistaken."

"You wrote a book."

"Still not famous."

"They are watching us," Rubberneck quavered. "I have proof."

"Stop rubbernecking and let me do my job."

"If Ubervich sees you writing in that notebook..."

With a sudden look of horror, Rubberneck dashed back behind his cubicle when Diane Ubervich appeared from seemingly nowhere. Lydia looked up and discovered her horn-rimmed boss dumping a massive pile of paperwork in front of her, which landed on her desk with a thud.

"Lindsay," Ubervich said with a scowl.

"Lydia."

"You are not going anywhere until this pile of paper is processed."

"But," Lydia stammered, "this will take me until at least midnight..."

"When one decides to blow off an entire morning of productive work hours..."

"Hunter..."

"... one makes up for lost time."

"My husband had something special planned..."

Ubervich raised her sanctimonious eyebrows nearly to her hairline.

"Can I come in early tomorrow or something?"

"Are you being insolent?"

"Ms. Ubervich, these are unusual circumstances," Lydia said, fidgeting. Intense people often made her shut down and she was courageously resisting the urge. "I mean it's not every day a person launches a debut novel. Hunter couldn't make it. He's going to make it up to me..."

"You are a ballsy little thing, aren't you?" Ubervich said with a curled lip. "You aren't leaving this desk until..."

"Can I at least go pee?"

"Are you being serious right now?"

Lydia blinked.

"You *go pee* more often than is seemly," Ubervich said as sharply as a malevolent porcupine needle. "As it happens, one's urinary compulsions are affecting one's productivity."

Lydia blinked.

"RUN!" Rubberneck screamed from his cubicle.

CHAPTER FOUR

Lydia did not, in fact, have to pee, nor did she have a so-called urinary compulsion. She simply needed a sanity break. One of many. Taking refuge in the public restroom, Lydia quite literally bumped into a scruffy lady who was cleaning toilets.

"Eliza!" Lydia apologetically uttered.

"Mind's somewhere else today, is it, Dear?"

"*'The devil is an ass. I do acknowledge it.'* ...Jonson."

"Don't tell me. I've got this one," Eliza said, raising a weathered index finger. "Diane Ubervich."

"What gave it away? The devil or the ass?"

"What did she do this time?" Eliza asked, putting down her toilet scrubber and wedging a fist in her hip.

"She's insane," Lydia stated the obvious.

"*'Who then is sane? He who is not a fool.'* ...Horace."

"*'The whole state is one vast insane asylum.'* ...Petigru."

"And they said our literature degrees wouldn't amount to anything," Eliza jibed.

"Remind me again why I am putting myself through this?" Lydia said, massaging her temples.

"Perk up, Kid. What you are and what you do are different things."

"Who said that?"

"I did," Eliza joked, nudging Lydia with a plunger. "Is that your new book?" Eliza asked, gesturing towards the book Lydia was holding; the one originally intended to butter up her boss.

"You know about my book?"

"I follow you on Instagram."

"Have you read it?"

"Me? Nah. Don't get paid until next Friday."

"Here," Lydia said, handing the book to Eliza.

Twittering happily, Eliza opened the novel. She was slightly disappointed to see that the book was autographed for Diane Ubervich, albeit with the name crossed out with an angry red pen.

Lydia gasped a little when she remembered the inscription.

"I'm touched," Eliza said, putting a reassuring hand on Lydia's shoulder. "Ubervich wouldn't have liked it anyway. The book's not about *her*."

"Sorry about that," Lydia said sheepishly.

"Hey, I'm just flattered you thought of me at all. Most people around here don't even realize I can read."

With a grunt, Eliza unceremoniously yanked a plunger out of a toilet. Lydia winced at the *shlumpf* noise it made.

"What did the human Norovirus do this time?" Eliza asked.

"My book launch was this morning," Lydia sighed. "And now Ubervich is taking disciplinary action. She is so emotionally disconnected from…" Lydia gestured vaguely.

"Never mind her," Eliza said, waving her hands around for effect. "Focus on what's important. You freaking did it, Kiddo. You launched your first novel. And everyone that matters gives a frig about that. How about Hunter? Bet he's bragging to everyone he knows about his brilliant, accomplished wifey."

"He couldn't make it."

"Shame."

"I was really disappointed."

"If it was humanly possible for him to be there, you know he would have been. He is batshit in love with you… Sorry, Dear… *Apeshit* in love."

Lydia pursed her lips. She knew Eliza was right. Hunter was quite literally the best thing that ever happened to her. He was brilliant. Magnetic. And he was so perfectly opposite to her in every way, which was exactly the balance she needed. Whenever Lydia got overwhelmed when the world got too *peopley,* Hunter stabilized her with his irresistible social skills. When Lydia's imagination carried her away, Hunter would carry her back with his level-headedness. If Lydia felt awkward, Hunter's effortless charm would make her feel like the most poised creature on the planet. He was affectionate. Patient. Loving. Wise.

Lydia felt like a selfish cad for letting Hunter's absence that day dampen her mood. Intellectually she knew it was impossible for him to attend her launch. A man cannot physically be in two places at once. Hunter made countless sacrifices for her so making this one, solitary sacrifice for him should not be a cause for drama or self-pity. No. Hunter had been nothing but supportive of her ambitions so Lydia would just have to regard this as an opportunity to support Hunter in his.

"He promised he'd make it up to me," Lydia said bashfully.

"Ooooo, Girl!" Eliza squealed.

"He left a message for me at work saying that he had something special planned."

"Hunter's surprises are always epic."

"But Ubervich is holding me hostage with a stack of paperwork the size of Kilimanjaro."

"Oh for the luvva..."

"Poor Hunter. I feel so bad about this. Especially since we didn't have a chance to celebrate today like we planned. I'm going to ruin everything."

"Maybe whatever he planned can wait, Dear."

"Knowing him, he probably hired a woodwind quartet. Or rented a thousand live doves to be released upon my arrival. Or arranged for Andrew Lloyd Webber to personally serenade me with the entire *Phantom* libretto."

"Then you better get back to work so as not to keep that dashing and strangely conscientious man waiting," Eliza winked.

CHAPTER FIVE

A faint hint of rosemary lingered in the air. Lydia exhaled for a solid fifteen seconds, knowing perfectly well in that moment, that she had ruined what was probably a perfectly romantic meal. Prepared by a practically perfect man who she obviously did not deserve right now.

"Hunter," Lydia said with her voice cracking from sheer exhaustion, "I am so sorry."

Completely unperturbed and oddly energetic despite the hour, Hunter swooped into the foyer and scooped Lydia into his arms.

"I missed you," he puckered. "Come on, Girl. Plant one on me. I've been waiting all day."

"You're supposed to be mad at me," Lydia said, snuggling into Hunter's chest.

"Enough of this squishy business. Sit."

Lydia observed that Hunter had prepared an extremely romantic spread intended for an exquisite meal. For two.

"I've ruined dinner," Lydia guessed.

"It's common knowledge that duck tastes better reheated," Hunter winked as he pulled out a chair for Lydia.

"Duck?" Lydia said sheepishly. "You went to so much trouble."

"Here's a drib of Merlot for my queen bee," Hunter said, concentrating intently on the wine he was pouring into Lydia's glass. "Now you stay here while I get the Parisian potatoes from the microwave."

Lydia involuntarily started to ugly cry.

"Baby, no," Hunter said. "Don't do that. Not now. I made duck."

"I ruined your perfect dinner."

"Hey, it's not ruined. I mean the candles have been burning a while and now they're kind of stumpy. But other than that..."

"I hate my boss."

"Everybody does," he said, prancing swiftly to the kitchen. "Hold on. I've got some rosemary drizzle on the stove."

"No, Hunter. Please. Sit."

"Sitting."

"I don't think I can do this anymore."

"Do what?"

"This," Lydia said, gesturing vaguely. "Everything. Ubervich. The lunatic who sits next to me, whatever his name is. Those flickering lights and asylum green walls..."

"Hey, hey, hey. Listen to me, Baby. This is all temporary, do you hear me? Everything. All of this. The job. This squingy apartment..."

"I'm feeling so uninspired," Lydia sniffled. "I think I'm losing myself..."

"Let's just forget about all that tonight, okay, Babe? We have so much to celebrate."

Lydia broke down into even more unattractive sobs.

"Baby?"

"I hate the city," Lydia said with her hands flailing for whatever reason. "I don't fit in anywhere. Nobody cares about anything. I've never felt so utterly disconnected from mankind. I mean the other day I was musing on the human condition..."

"No, Lyds. What did I tell you about musing on the human condition? It always makes you cry. Please stop."

"I can't help it, Hunter. Here I am in the most peopled city in Canada and I feel totally alone out there. Which is insane, right? Because there's literally more people than I can emotionally tolerate sometimes and here I am with the best man ever. I mean look at you with those violet bedroom eyes and the... I don't know... face. I really like your face, Hunter. So it's totally not your fault I feel this way because you are basically a god..."

"Babe..."

"And it's not like I don't have friends. Today for example, I went to *The Refined Cucumber* with Meredith, Patrice and Jules..."

"Why?"

"What do you mean, why? They've been my friends since high school."

"Aren't they a little out of your league?"

"Hey!"

"You know what I mean, Lyds. They're... I don't know. Lofty. Posh. Primped. You're stressing yourself out trying to keep up with them."

"Are you saying," Lydia said, twiddling a strand of her long, mousy hair, "I'm not..."

"Don't put words in my mouth, Babe. You know how much I enjoy looking at you. I'm just trying to say they may be holding you to a standard that you just can't... Didn't they bully you in high school?"

"People can change," Lydia sniffled. "We reconnected on Facebook and now they think I'm cool."

"But they are so different from you, Lyds. Maybe if you found some friends who are more like you..."

"Literally nobody is like me, Hunter. I'm atypical."

"Well, there's that."

"Hunter, I think I'm reaching a breaking point..."

"Drizzle!" Hunter blurted suddenly as he leaped in the air in a manner that was not unlike a Gene Kelly musical theatre number.

Hunter rushed into the kitchen and returned shortly with a smoking saucepan.

"Needless calories, really," Hunter said blithely. "I've heard naked duck is the way to go anyway."

"Hunter," Lydia said with a quiet, emotional rasp. "Is it bad that I don't feel like celebrating right now?"

Hunter protruded a lower lip sympathetically and blanketed Lydia in his arms.

"Anything you need, Baby," Hunter breathed into her ear.

***

Lydia felt like an extremely loved enchilada, lying in bed with Hunter's arms still wrapped around her. He had fallen asleep like a normal person about six hours ago. Lydia on the other hand, had been awake all night and by now, her eyes looked like a pair of bulging, sleep deprived cherry tomatoes. Her eyes stung as she blinked at her clock. She wondered if an existential crisis was a legitimate reason to call in sick for work.

She heard a sound that might have been her cell phone. But that would be absurd, given the obnoxious time of day. She was only vaguely aware that 5:30 came twice a day. She did not recognize the incoming phone number. Being delirious with exhaustion, she answered anyway.

"Hello?" Lydia said, answering her cell in a sleepy tone, three octaves lower than normal.

"Lydia Knapp?" said an unfamiliar, caffeine-charged voice coming out of her phone.

"One and the same," Lydia yawned.

"I apologize for the ridiculous hour," the voice said. "I wanted to get in touch with you before anyone else had a chance. Did I wake you?"

Lydia shook her head, too groggy to realize that the man on the phone could not actually see her.

"The name's Floyd Tifford," the voice explained. "My nephew met you at the launch of your debut novel, *Fairweather Friends Forever*. You might remember him. Gangly lad? Ardent? Answers to the name of Logan?"

"Uncle Floyd?" Lydia said with a nauseated twinge in her voice.

"Logan may have mentioned to you his intentions of showing me your book."

"He did."

"I loved it, Lydia. Couldn't put it down."

"Okay..."

"Mildew. Classic."

"Floyd..."

"I want to meet you."

"You do?"

"You are exactly what I'm looking for."

"Wait..."

"When I see something I like, I just go for it."

"I'm really not interested."

"Can I get you a coffee? Say around seven-thirty-ish?"

"I don't think that's appropriate."

"Herbal tea then? I'm not an unreasonable man."

"I don't want to."

"I don't understand."

"What, you've never been turned down before?"

"Generally, no."

"Wow."

"Normally authors *want* publishing deals."

"Well I'm not... what?"

"*Tifford & Fudd* has been known to scout some of the best up and coming talent."

"*Tifford & Fudd?*... Oh God..."

"Are you under contract with another company or..."

"Holy frig…"

"Ms. Knapp?"

"I mean yes."

"Yes? Yes, you are currently under contract? Or yes, you would like to set up a meeting?"

"I… uh… where do I go? To meet you?"

"Perky's Espresso Bar. I'll be the one who smells distinctly of cigars and wearing a corduroy fedora."

"I love corduroy fedoras. I own one."

"Excellent. Bye now."

Lydia's hand trembled and seemed physically incapable of putting down the phone.

"Hunter?" Lydia whispered while trying to nudge Hunter awake. "You're not going to believe this. Hunter?"

Hunter was clearly marooned somewhere in the Southern Hemisphere of Dreamland. Lydia pursed her lips. She did not have the heart to wake him after he had waited up late for her to come home, only to stay awake well into night, trying to comfort Lydia while she was in the throes of an emotional meltdown. Instead, she scribbled a note for him and left it on the pillow.

"Hunter… Best news ever! Meeting with Tifford & Fudd. For reals! Couldn't bear to wake you – you're so cute when you're asleep. Talk later. Kisses… Lyds."

CHAPTER SIX

Askew from a helter-skelter bike ride through the unreasonably congested streets of Toronto, Lydia burst indelicately through the doors of Perky's Esspresso Bar. Collecting herself as though she had intended to resemble a blustering weather front with a strand of hair stuck in her mouth, Lydia scanned the room for a corduroy fedora and subtly sniffed the air for cigars.

At the corner table sat a slightly pedantic looking bloke in a moss green, tweed jacket. He resembled the images Lydia found online during her Google searches. Either this was Floyd Tifford or a particularly adroit impersonator.

Lydia ambled towards Tifford's table, spitting the strand of stray hair from her mouth and adjusting her paisley, boho tunic. Also her corduroy fedora because it never hurts to make a stylistic impression. She awkwardly waved when Tifford lolled his eyeballs in her direction, and then gestured with a cordial nod for her to take the seat next to his.

"Lydia Knapp?" Tifford said extending a hand for her to shake.

"Yes, Sir," Lydia said breathlessly, taking a seat.

"So glad you could make it on such short notice."

"Pleasure," Lydia said, wishing her heart would stop thumping like a nervous bongo drum.

"Fairweather Friends Forever," Tifford continued, lowering his glasses to the end of his nose while skimming through Lydia's novel. "Original. Yet relatable. These characters are so vivid and quirky."

"Vivid and quirky," Lydia said awkwardly. "That's me."

"Indeed," Tifford said with a smirk. "Yours is a unique voice that deserves a chance to be heard."

Lydia swallowed hard.

"I'm sure you are aware of Corrina Featherbottom? Sven Eklund? Orly Renfrew?"

Lydia nodded.

"Each of them bestselling authors. Featherbottom was this year's recipient of the Giller Prize. She's ours. I discovered her at an open mic thing in the Annex. I have a keen eye for new talent, and I have a hunch you could be the next Corrina Featherbottom. My hunches are rarely, if ever wrong, Lydia Knapp."

Lydia nodded more circularly and with wider eyes.

"Do you think you could crank out another one of these?" Tifford asked, waving his copy of Lydia's novel in front of her as though teasing a puppy with a chewy liver treat. "Except, you know. Completely different?"

"I... think so?"

"By September?"

Lydia's mouth moved around for a while, trying to find words.

"What's going on with your face right now?" Tifford asked dryly.

"September?"

"Is that a problem?"

"It's just... it took me three years and eleven months to write *Fairweather Friends Forever.*"

"And... your publisher was okay with that?"

"I sort of wrote it first and then pitched it to Pussywillow Press."

"That's not how it works in the business, Lydia. We have to move things along. Deadlines and all that."

"But this is April."

"You're not Lydia anymore?"

"The month. Not me."

"Sven Eklund wrote *Love Odyssey of a Lumberjack* in less than three months. And his book was featured on *Breakfast Television with Raj & Gert.*"

"It's just... my process..."

"Aw jeez. You have a *process?* You're not one of those flakes who ghosts the publisher for a year while you sit around waiting for your muse?"

"I have a day job," Lydia explained sheepishly. "I generally only have an hour or so each night to write and it's challenging to concentrate with all the road noise outside my apartment…"

"Let me get this straight," Tifford said, trying to shake the disbelief from his head. "You basically need four years…"

"Minus one month."

"Listen, Lydia. I think you've got what it takes but if you can't treat this like a professional gig…"

"I want to, it's just…"

"Are you turning down my offer?"

"No! It's just my job…"

"Quit."

"I need the income…"

"I'm offering you a job here! *Tifford & Fudd* is the third biggest publisher in the country. Do you understand the volume of books…"

"But how will I eat or pay rent between now and September?"

"Let me get this straight. You basically can't *afford* to have a decent paying job? With fame and all that attached?"

Lydia gaped.

"I need a cigar," Tifford said, screeching his chair across the floor as he made an abrupt exodus.

CHAPTER SEVEN

She was only eleven minutes late.

Lydia darted into the office and made a beeline for her cubicle. Alas, she was intercepted by the horn-rimmed eyes of her vehement boss who was doing a convincing impersonation of a punitive sturgeon.

"Does one need to buy one a watch?" Ubervich said with the cadence of a vice principal at a school for delinquents.

"I had a meeting with a publisher..."

"I was on the phone with India this morning."

"The country?"

"When you didn't show up for work, I assumed you were putting your position up for grabs."

"I'm *eleven* minutes late."

"They said they would be happy to replace you."

"India said that?"

"Are you trying to be funny?"

"Actually, no."

"Pack your things."

"What are you..."

"Are you daft?"

"I..."

"The word is *fired,* Laura."

"Lydia."

"Doesn't make much difference now, does it?"

At a loss for words as Diane Ubervich sauntered from the room, Lydia gaped stupidly, seemingly stapled to the obsolete carpet. The intense face of Rubberneck peered around the corner of his cubicle, staring at Lydia forebodingly like a damned soul. Lydia could feel his stare burning the back of her head.

"Piss off, you freak show," Lydia spat.

Startled, Rubberneck quickly ducked back into his cubicle.

***

Sniffling profusely and wiping tears with her sleeve, Lydia locked herself in a bathroom stall. She was just about to call Hunter when she noticed he had already left her a text.

"I owe you a celebration. Meet me tonight after work. Chez Raoul. 8:30. This will be the best night of your life. Promise... Hunter."

Chez Raoul? Hunter really outdid himself this time. Lydia was humbled by how hard Hunter was trying to make it up to her for missing her launch. Lydia bit her quivering lip, feeling humiliated about calling Hunter now. How could she break the news of losing her job when he was so clearly proud of her? Sure, Hunter would be supportive no matter what. But she felt like such a loser. Lydia legitimately struggled with the notion of shattering Hunter's delusions of her being a genius.

Should she call Meredith, Patrice or Jules instead? Or would that be even more treacherous than calling Hunter? Lydia had somehow managed to win the favor of the three most enviable girls from high school. Even though she knew they genuinely regarded her as part of their elite group, a nagging feeling made Lydia wonder if their acceptance of her was hinging on her *not* being a pathetic dud. Or maybe that was just the social anxiety telling lies to her brain. Either way, Lydia was not about to take any chances.

Lydia curled into a ball atop a toilet and wept audibly.

"Knock, knock?" Eliza tried.

The stall door creaked open, revealing Lydia's tear-steaked visage.

"Love..." Eliza said maternally.

"I hate this city," Lydia snuffed with an unfortunate string of snot steaming from her nostril. "I hate this job. I hate this... I just hate this."

"Come here," Eliza said tenderly, gesturing for Lydia to find sanctuary in her matronly arms.

"Sometimes I think I'm the only reasonable person in this city," Lydia snuffed. "Like everyone around me has completely taken leave of their senses. Which is asinine I know. Seeing as how I'm the one losing my marbles."

"I know," Eliza soothed.

"Why do I have to be so rational?" Lydia asked irrationally. "If I could just stop caring so much, maybe I'd fit in somewhere."

"People care," Eliza assured her. "Just not about *each other.*"

"I feel so isolated!" Lydia sighed. "This city can be so lonely."

"Shhh..."

"Ubervich is the craziest of them all," Lydia chuffed. "You know what she just did?"

"She canned you?"

"How could you possibly know that?"

"When you've been scrubbing johns as long as I have, you learn to read people."

"I feel so incapable," Lydia moaned. "I can't make a real go at writing. I can't even hold down a low skilled job."

"'*The mind of man is capable of anything because everything is in it.*' ...Conrad."

Lydia blew her nose.

"Your turn," Eliza nudged.

"What?" Lydia whimpered. "Oh. Um… *"Here in your mind, you have complete privacy…"'*

"'…Here, there's no difference between what is and what could be.' …Palahniuk."

"I'm really going to miss that."

"Me too, Dear."

Lydia's cell phone rang inconveniently.

"It's Hunter," Lydia quavered.

"Better answer it."

"I can't."

"You can't keep this from your husband."

Reluctantly, Lydia answered.

"Hello?"

"Lyds!" Hunter said with explosive joy on the phone. "Did you get my text?"

"… yep."

"Okay, so you're cool with Chez Raoul? You're not going to be held up at work again, are you? Because tonight is the night we celebrate. No fair reneging, okay?"

"I am very sure I won't be late… Can we even afford Chez Raoul?"

"You let me worry about whether we can afford it. It's a special occasion with my special girl. It's going to be epic."

"I'll be there then."

"I can't wait. Bye, Babe."

Triangulating an eyebrow, Lydia gawked at her phone.

"And?" Eliza said expectantly.

"How are we supposed to afford Chez Raoul? Their pre-dinner baguette costs more than my refrigerator."

"Blimey!" Eliza said, clutching her chest. "That romantic soul is trying so hard to make you feel special."

"I know but the timing is terrible!" Lydia squeaked. "All in one day I managed to get fired AND screw up a life-altering publishing deal. Now we're going to a restaurant not even Bono can afford so he can demonstrate how proud he is of me? Gah! This whole thing is ridiculous. I'm just going to quit writing and become a shepherd."

"'All great deeds and all great thoughts have ridiculous beginnings,'" Eliza said wryly.

"Camus," Lydia pouted.

"That's my girl."

Impulsively, Lydia gave Eliza a fervent, good-bye squeeze.

"I don't know what I'll do without you, Eliza."

While hugging Lydia, Eliza replied stoically, *"'Fill your paper with the breathings of your heart.'* …Wordsworth."

CHAPTER EIGHT

Lydia felt woefully underdressed when she awkwardly trudged into Chez Raoul. The sleeves of her boho tunic were stained with snot from wiping her weepy nose all day. Too embarrassed to return home, Lydia spent the harrowing daylight hours traipsing aimlessly around Toronto. And now her pointless procrastination was about to come to a screeching halt.

Hunter spotted her from across the room. His face was beaming like a ridiculous sun. So bright was his aura that Lydia found herself squinting as though emerging out of a dark room. Hunter's eyes were focused solely on Lydia, as though everything in the room other than her had dematerialized.

Embarrassed, Lydia gestured to her tunic which was not only snotty, but by now also smelled like Toronto.

"Don't worry about that," Hunter winked as he handed Lydia a garment bag. "I bought you something special to wear."

"Hunter..."

"Open this." Hunter begged.

Slowly, Lydia unzipped the garment bag and peaked inside.

"Hunter, no..."

"Put it on in the ladies' room."

"Hunter, we can't afford…"

"It's okay, Babe. Go on."

Reluctantly, Lydia went to the ladies' room to change into the opulent, emerald green evening dress Hunter gave her. She winced as she checked the tag. Lydia had never worn anything with a designer label. The price of the dress, had Lydia been aware of it, would have given her a cluster headache. She wriggled into the dress, feeling somewhat like she was molding her body into a mermaid fin. Which would have been a glorious feeling, had she been a mermaid. But in that moment, she felt more like a flounder.

Scrutinizing herself in the mirror, Lydia felt guilty on many levels. Firstly, she had no right to wear something this expensive. The money would be better spent on feeding starving orphans or sponsoring a nice refugee. She could not help but feel disappointed that Hunter apparently had no idea how much she was sickened by the color emerald green. How could she be so entitled as to wish he had splurged for a comely earth tone? Or a rust color if he was feeling crazy? The important thing was that he went out of his way to impress her. Stewing over the fact that Hunter had forgotten her color preferences would make her incredibly ungrateful. Nope. She was not *that girl*.

When Lydia emerged from the ladies' room, Hunter was waiting expectantly. His violet eyes were utterly mesmerized as Lydia literally glistened in the ambient light.

"You're perfect," Hunter said with a twinkly smile. Seriously, where did this guy buy his toothpaste?

"If you say so," Lydia said self-consciously.

"The color…"

"Yes…" Lydia said with a gurgle of illness in her voice. "The… color."

Once seated, Lydia took a sip of wine and was startled by how much better it tasted than cheap wine.

"So we're finally doing this," Hunter said giddily. "I told you I had something special planned, did I not?"

"You did in fact say that," Lydia nodded awkwardly. "You really went all out."

"We have lots to celebrate."

Lydia smiled bashfully.

"There was something I didn't get around to saying last night…"

"Sorry about that."

"Don't be sorry, Lyds," Hunter said, cupping his hand over hers. "It's just, this is a momentous occasion, and I wanted the moment to be perfect when I tell you this."

"Momentous?" Lydia laughed nervously. "It was just a limited print run but thank you."

Hunter blinked.

"Okay…" Hunter continued, still blinking with perplexity. "So here's the news. Do you want to hear the news?"

"Wait, news?"

"You're not going to believe this…"

"Are you pregnant?"

"No, Lyds."

"Am I?"

"I don't think so."

"Then?"

"Yesterday," Hunter said, taking a deep breath, "I got a massive promotion."

"You… got a promotion."

"I was in negotiations all day yesterday…"

"Which is why you missed my launch," Lydia nodded.

"I knew you'd understand, Babe. See, I'm going to be representing my company at all the international conferences. I convinced them that I would be the most capable of persuasively presenting our new brand of industrial plastic to the global population. And I'll be reporting directly to the CEO."

Lydia gaped.

"And the pay increase," Hunter beamed. "Sweet God! It's going to be a game changer for us, Babe… Babe?"

"I… nothing."

"It's not nothing, Lyds. Tell me what's wrong."

"I just thought... I thought you were planning a special evening... because of my book."

Hunter's face deflated slowly like a remorseful helium balloon.

"... Oh," Hunter choked.

"Hunter, I'm sorry. I shouldn't have assumed..."

"Lyds, I suck. I was so caught up in the thrill of what was going on. I mean, industrial plastic is my life. I wanted this so bad..."

"I'm happy for you," Lydia blinked. "I really am, Hunter. You work so hard."

"I'm going to make it up to you," Hunter said with epiphany.

"Hunter, you really don't have to..."

"My new position requires me to travel," Hunter began.

Lydia suddenly turned greener than her dress.

"I'll take you with me!" Hunter said with a clap of revelation.

"On a business trip?" Lydia asked, her lip curling with uncertainty.

"We'll make it romantic. California. New York. China. Belgium. I have associates in all those places. You pick."

Lydia resisted the urge to hyperventilate.

"Babe, this promotion is the best thing that's ever..."

"Hunter," Lydia said quickly, "I lost my job today."

"Perfect!" Hunter blurted obliviously.

Lydia gaped.

"What?" Hunter laughed nervously.

"I also turned down a publishing opportunity."

"You had a publishing opportunity?"

"I left you a note on your pillow."

"You said you were meeting with *Tifford & Fudd.*"

"That's a publisher."

"I thought it was like two of your friends. You have really weird friends, Lyds."

"How could you not know..."

"Why in the world would you turn down a publishing deal?"

"They wanted me to have a book finished by September."

"And?"

"And that's impossible given my lack of time."

"What lack of time? You're unemployed!" Hunter said a little too joyfully.

"Hunter, my bruised dignity..."

"Lyds, that job was beneath you and you know it."

"I failed at something I was largely overqualified for. Do you not see how disgraceful that is?"

"Will you please just swallow your pride and look at this as a unique opportunity? You can write full time now. I can support you."

Lydia bit her lip, looking slightly ill.

CHAPTER NINE

Hunter had a good point. His promotion was indeed life-changing for both of them. For the first time since she was a dependent in her parents' home, Lydia could actually afford to write full-time in the comfort of her own apartment. And upon further reflection, Lydia realized that the universe was clearly sending her a signal that now was the time to move forward instead of running without a destination in the hamster wheel of subsistence.

After careful consideration, she took Floyd Tifford up on his offer and found herself contractually bound to a September deadline for a brand new novel. She really hoped she could live up to Tifford's expectations. She had not worked with a deadline since she wrote a comparative essay for her Canadian Literature class in university. The topic was: *Comparing the Literary Significance of the Letter R in the Early Works of Michael Ondaatje and Robertson Davies.* Not that it matters. But Lydia was quite proud of that essay.

With Hunter away on a business trip, the apartment was weirdly hollow. Not quiet by any means, seeing as how the apartment was in the heart of a bustling, deafening city. But eerily solitary. Each morning she would grab a mug of instant coffee, set up her laptop at the narrow, kitchen table and turn on the kitchen faucet. She could not concentrate unless the faucet was running.

Water inspired her and since she lived nowhere near the harbor, the faucet would have to do.

Sadly, each day Lydia would face a plethora of interruptions, including but not limited to the barking Pekinese next door. While Lydia tried to complain to her neighbor about the verbose dog, the neighbor argued that the Pekinese had never been a problem before – most likely because Lydia had never worked from home before.

Likewise, Lydia was interrupted by a wailing toddler who showed up at her door, claiming to have lost his apartment. When Lydia tried to ask the tot questions pertaining to his parental situation, the child informed her that he was not allowed to talk to strangers. Lydia asked the boy why he would therefore approach Lydia, her being a stranger and all that. To which the tot replied, *'because everyone else in the building has jobs.'*

Naturally, Meredith, Patrice and Jules showed up on a regular basis, seeing as how Lydia *wasn't busy.* Jules, being Jules, often brought over trendy, Icelandic take-out and would habitually ask Lydia if she would prefer fava bean paste or lotus mustard with her skyr and fermented shark. The fishy smell would linger in her poorly ventilated apartment long after her oblivious friends left, rendering it impossible to focus.

A window washer took a particular interest in Lydia while ogling her from outside on his scaffold.

Frequent jackhammers, sirens and honking horns would often make Lydia reach for some pain killers.

And of course, the couple next door decided to start having domestic disputes on an ongoing basis, regarding some guy named Pablo and his avocados. Time after time, Lydia would bang on the wall, threatening to involve the police.

Nights were even worse for Lydia. Her senses were heightened after dark, making every ambient noise outside seem like it was amplified like a death metal base guitar. She would hug Hunter's pillow for comfort, squishing herself into a ball of anxiety.

This was clearly not working.

***

Jetlagged, Hunter flung his carryon luggage on the linoleum and squinted around the room for Lydia.

"Babe?" he yawned.

No answer.

After a brief scan around the room, Hunter found a stiff, comatose version of Lydia sitting at the kitchen table.

"Are you okay?" Hunter asked tentatively.

Lydia slowly turned to face Hunter with her lifeless, bloodshot eyes bulging like a zombified mannequin.

"Pablo," Lydia said lifelessly. "Avocados."

"Why is the faucet running?"

"Water," Lydia said monotonically. "Need. Inspiration."

"Whoa," Hunter said, sliding into the seat next to Lydia. "you look like garbage."

"Thanks for that."

"Dead garbage. If that's a thing."

"Hunter, this isn't going to work out."

"What do you mean?" Hunter asked, snarfing a breakfast biscuit from Lydia's plate.

"I have to get out of here."

"Aren't you going to ask about my trip?"

"The city is ending me."

"I mean, I was gone for a week."

"Hunter..."

"Okay fine. We'll make this about you."

"Excuse me?"

Hunter made a *never mind* gesture by wagging his biscuit in the air.

"I'm struggling, Hunter. We need to talk about this."

"Did you finish your book?"

"In one week?"

"Hey man, I don't know how the process goes."

"Do you have any comprehension of what I've been through this week?"

"So you weren't productive? After a week of having nothing else to do?"

"Let me see," said Lydia sarcastically. "Between the jackhammers, the Pekinese, the scaffold perv and the lotus mustard..."

"I don't follow..."

"No, Hunter. I have not been productive. And I won't be productive until I am liberated from the Seventh Circle of Hell."

"The..."

"Toronto."

"I might have a solution."

"Tell me."

"I'm going to Shanghai."

"ARE YOU FREAKING KIDDING ME?"

"Babe..."

"You're leaving me again? How is that a solution?"

"You're not understanding me, Babe..."

"My social anxiety is getting out of control in this dense, urban population! All these people... these totally disconnected people are giving me the shakes! Look at me, Hunter! I'm shaking! Without you here I can't..."

"You can come with me!"

Lydia gaped.

"Babe?"

"With you."

"That's right."

"To Shanghai."

"Great idea, eh?"

"As in the most populated city in China."

"For six months!"

Lydia gaped.

"Please stop gaping, Lyds."

"So your solution to my social anxiety – induced by living in the city – is to go to a bigger city?"

"You make it sound like a bad thing."

"I don't believe this," Lydia said, shaking her head. "Do you even know me at all?"

"So... you don't want to go."

"I want to go somewhere more remote. Not to a place that has an official person who's paid to squish people into subways."

"I don't want to leave you for six months," Hunter sulked.

"And I don't want you to leave, obviously."

"What are you proposing, exactly? Are you saying you want to move?"

"There's no reason for me to be in the city anymore. I have no job tying me down here. You're never home anymore…"

Hunter buried his face in his hands, trying to process.

"Hunter?" Lydia tried.

"Where is it that you want to go?" Hunter asked, muffled.

"I don't know," Lydia sighed. "Somewhere secluded. With water."

"Water…"

"Water inspires me."

"Industrial plastic inspires me," Hunter muttered. "Not that you'd care…"

"Hunter, I know this would be a big change and that you're more of a city guy. But there is no way in Hell I'll be able to finish writing a novel by September if I'm cooped up in this urban nightmare. Can you ponder that for a moment? My career won't go anywhere if I don't drastically change my context. Toronto his holding me back. Can't you see that?"

"I'm supposed to be comfortable leaving you in the remote wilderness for months at a time? Alone?"

"I don't belong here, Hunter," Lydia said solemnly.

The silence that followed made Lydia feel a stress rash form on her face.

CHAPTER TEN

Lydia and Hunter jostled in the backseat of their real estate agent's bluish Hyundai as they ventured down a gravelly, rural road. Lydia curiously peered out the side window at the dense forest of conifers that lined the road as it led them into the arcane depths of wilderness. Not a soul had she seen for the past seventy-five minutes at least, save for a traumatized squirrel dashing across the road, apparently never having seen a motor vehicle in his furry, little life.

Not a trace of civilization could be seen anywhere.

Trees.

So many trees.

"Where are we going, exactly?" Hunter asked, craning his neck to get a glimpse of what may have been a rotting, abandoned hunting shack.

"Elsewhere," Brent the real estate agent said, swerving around a sharp bend.

"Obviously," Hunter said, gripping the armrests paranoidly. "I haven't seen a town limit sign in over two hours."

"That's because Elsewhere is not on the map," Brent said, briefly consulting handwritten directions on a piece of paper. "I can't even plunk the coordinates into my GPS."

"I'm confused," Hunter grimaced.

"Elsewhere," Brent explained. "The name of the region we're in right now. It's an undesignated area. On the outskirts of rural Quebec, but it's so remote, that neither Ontario nor Quebec claimed it."

"Elsewhere," Hunter said, unimpressed. "Never heard of it."

"That's the appeal," Brent nodded. "You asked for something secluded so this could be exactly what you're looking for. Not a chance of it being developed, seeing as it is not officially part of any particular province. Besides, not many people would bother driving this far from civilization, regardless of how peaceful it is."

"I'm excited," Lydia said giddily.

Hunter looked at Lydia as though she was green.

"Any special reason you want to find a place as secluded as this?" Brent asked, craning his neck from the front seat. "I understand you want to work remotely but this..."

"I need absolute quiet and tranquility in order to focus."

"What line of work are you in?"

"I'm a writer."

"Intriguing! Is she any good?" Brent asked Hunter with a playful jerk of his head.

"I've heard only complimentary things about her new book."

"Wait," Lydia interjected. "You haven't read it?"

"Babe," Hunter chuckled awkwardly, "when would I have time…"

"Not even on the plane or…"

"Lyds," Hunter said discreetly through the side of his mouth, "let's keep it real. Reading is kind of a niche thing. When have you ever seen me with a book? Grownups don't have time to fritter around."

Lydia blinked a stinging tear from her eye.

"Just kidding," Hunter jibed.

Lydia blinked harder.

"You know I'm kidding, right, Lyds?"

"I shouldn't have assumed…"

"I'll read your book, I will."

"You will?"

"As soon as I have time."

***

The car door slamming shut was literally the only sound. It made a cluster of nervous birds scatter. When Lydia emerged from Brent's car, her eyes glossed with wonder. She instantly dashed around the property, absorbing her surroundings. A ramshackle cottage stood atop a rocky hillock, composed of rugged Canadian Shield. The walls were splintery but oozed with character. A rusty swing hung from the rickety porch, just waiting for Lydia to laze on it. A stone chimney peeped out of the roof, threatening to crumble, but stoically it still stood proud. Lydia imagined wispy plumes of smoke twirling out of it on a crisp, autumn morning.

Mature cedars adorned the property, jutting angularly out of the rocky hillock. The ground was carpeted with orange pine needles and Lydia relished the sound they made beneath her feet. A worn path led her down to the waterfront, where she was greeted by a vast, glassy lake. The fluttering, lime green spring leaves on the birch trees reflected off the lake like a winsome watercolor painting.

The water was eerily still.

"And this is what I fight for," Lydia thought to herself, *"the freedom of the mind to take any direction it wishes'... Steinbeck."*

"Lovesick Lake," Brent said, ambling down to the waterfront with his hands in the pockets of his windbreaker jacket. "What do you think?"

"Lovesick Lake?" Lydia pondered. "What a poetic name. Hunter, what do you think?"

"Epically poetic," Hunter grumbled, slapping a blackfly on the back of his neck."

"Gorgeous view of the waterfront," Brent said, launching into his sales pitch. "And before you ask, yes. There is indoor plumbing."

"It's so tranquil," Lydia sighed.

"Very," Brent nodded. "They say you can hear the mosquitos when they hit the water."

"Why are all these surrounding cabins boarded up?" Hunter asked critically.

"Property taxes spiked several years back," Brent explained. "While neither Ontario nor Quebec wanted to claim Elsewhere, neither province hesitated to exploit the residents with taxes. The folks here lived modest lives, see. So nobody could afford to pay taxes to two governments. Everybody just packed up and left, it seems."

"So I'd get the whole lake to myself?" Lydia asked hopefully.

"With the exception of that bloke across the lake," Brent said, pointing to a humble cottage in the distance. "An older man lives there but he pretty much keeps to himself. So he shouldn't disturb you or cause any problems."

"Hunter, I really like it here," Lydia said, practically bouncing.

"I don't know," Hunter winced, "I..."

"I feel like I belong here," Lydia begged.

"The idea of you being all alone," Hunter said grimly. "Like ALL alone out here. I'm going to be away so often..."

"I've never belonged anywhere before," Lydia said with tears practically forming on the brims of her eyelids. "This lake. I think it *wants* me."

Hunter's lips burbled defeatedly as he exhaled.

"You really want this, don't you," Hunter muttered.

"More than anything," Lydia pleaded.

"And this water," Hunter said, tilting Lydia's chin up, looking her in the eyes. "It's going to inspire you, right?"

"More than you can know!" Lydia said, her eyes brimming with hope.

"You won't be lonely?"

"The girls will visit me," Lydia replied. "Or I'll make friends with the guy across the lake if I get desperate."

"Amenities?" Hunter inquired.

"Elsewhere Township is a thirty-five minute drive from here," Brent said. "It's sparse, but you'll find all the basics you need. Only about twenty-five people live there, and I've heard they're a bit wary of outsiders. But you'll figure things out soon enough."

"Lydia can't drive."

"I have a bike."

"Wifi connection?" Hunter asked.

"Spotty," Brent admitted. "But it does the job so long as you don't need anything high speed. Or consistent. Or of ample quality. Bandwidth might be an issue. But other than that, yes."

"That's unacceptable," Hunter complained.

"Hunter," Lydia moaned. "That kind of thing doesn't matter to me. All I need is for my laptop to have power. I don't need the internet. Not every day at least."

"What if I need to get a hold of you via Skype or something?" Hunter asked. "I don't see any telephone wires anywhere…"

"It'll do, Hunter," Lydia said, slightly impatient. "I'm sure there's enough signal for us to communicate."

"You're sure you don't want to come to Shanghai with me?" Hunter asked, cupping Lydia's face.

"This feels like home, Hunter," Lydia said softly.

"You realize I'm going to be worried sick about you the whole time I'm gone…"

"Yes?" Lydia squealed. "Are you saying yes right now?"

Hunter groaned.

CHAPTER ELEVEN

Practically bouncing in her seat at *The Refined Cucumber,* Lydia percolated with glee as she described her new dream home to Meredith, Patrice and Jules. The lake. The cedars. The adorable, splintery cabin. The wildlife. The vivid color. The tranquility. The inspiration. Oh, the inspiration!

"Lovesick Lake?" Meredith said, curling her lips as though the word itself tasted like expired milk.

"It is literally a piece of Heaven," Lydia marveled. "No jackhammers. No yapping Pekinese..."

"No civilization..." muttered Meredith.

"We are SO going to miss you," pouted Patrice.

"Lunch will never be the same," Meredith said with a tone of impending doom.

"You're talking like I'm on my way to my own funeral," Lydia chortled. "It's not like we're never going to see each other again."

"We're going to be missing a side of our little triangle," Patrice lamented.

"Triangles have three sides, actually," Lydia pointed out.

"You promise you'll make frequent trips to the city?" Jules asked.

"You better!" Patrice said, pointing an artificially red fingernail at Lydia.

"I was thinking more along the lines of you guys visiting me at the lake."

Meredith, Patrice and Jules simultaneously goggled.

"Think about it," Lydia said excitedly. "A free retreat. A girls' weekend. Think of it as *self-care.*"

"Is there electricity?" Jules asked bluntly.

"Of course there's electricity, you goof," Lydia laughed. "I bought a cottage for God's sake. I didn't join a frigging missionary commune."

"Do you suppose there's squirrels?" Patrice asked ominously.

"I can pretty much guarantee it," answered Lydia.

Patrice pursed her lips with worry.

"Are you sure about this?" Meredith asked rationally. "I mean, you'll be missing out on all the nightlife."

"There's nightlife," Lydia said, not intending to sound offended. "Owls. Have you ever seen an actual owl before? And what about the stars? I don't think I've seen a star in my entire adult life. Until I was eleven, I thought smog was a shade of blue."

The girls shifted uncomfortably in their seats.

"Come on, you guys," Lydia whimpered. "I'll be all alone out there. You don't want me to be all alone, do you?"

The girls looked guiltily at each other.

"Sure, Doll," Meredith nodded uncertainly. "Your little hovel sounds perfectly charming. You name the time and the place, and we'll be... there."

CHAPTER TWELVE

Since the cabin had been unoccupied for nearly three years, the closing date was extremely flexible. Naturally, Lydia jumped at the chance to move in as soon as possible, especially with Hunter leaving for Shanghai one week after they viewed the property. So Lydia packed up her meager belongings within six days before making the trek back to Elsewhere.

The furniture was included with the cabin which made the move go much more swimmingly. Sure, the furniture was a little worse for wear, what with the conspicuous tear in the tweed couch, the scuffed kitchen table and the lopsided bed. But Lydia was more interested in charm and character than she was creature comforts, so these minor details did not bother her at all. In fact, she found the cabin's interior to be compellingly summer-campy.

"Can you identify that smell?" Hunter asked, squinching his nose as he carried in the last of Lydia's suitcases.

"It's the smell of a thousand stories," Lydia said dreamily. "Secrets that only this cabin will ever know. All the things it has seen but will never tell."

"Really," Hunter said dryly. "Because it smells a bit like toxic mold."

Lydia pulled a tweed curtain aside, revealing a panoramic view of Lovesick Lake. Given the vantage point of the cottage, she could see the occupied cottage across the lake. She could vaguely see a grizzled man with a hatchet, standing on his dock.

"Hunter, come here," Lydia coaxed.

Hunter obeyed, squinting at the hatchet-wielding figure in the distance.

"That him?" Hunter asked with a jerk of his head.

"He has a weird energy," Lydia pointed out.

"How can you possibly know that from so far away?"

"I can just tell," Lydia nodded seriously. "Maybe it's the hatchet, I don't know."

"Ignore him," Hunter advised.

"He should at least come over and introduce himself."

"On his own time. He doesn't strike me as the social type. Look at him."

"But I'm his only neighbor," Lydia pondered. "And I'm apparently the first neighbor he's had in three years."

"Which is likely why he lacks any social graces," Hunter concluded.

"I should bring him some muffins or something."

"Seriously?"

"We don't know his story, Hunter. Maybe he needs a friend. I might need a friend eventually. What if I need something while you're in Shanghai?"

"What if he's insane?"

"It is sometimes an appropriate response to reality to go insane... Dick."

"Who's Dick?"

"Philip K. Dick?"

Crickets.

"Valis?"

"You're making no sense right now."

"I was trying to say that the guy might not be as nefarious as you think. Maybe he's had a hard life or something."

"Then why didn't you just say that?"

"I was being poetic."

"By quoting some other guy? Doesn't sound too poetic to me."

Lydia blinked.

"Kidding," Hunter jibed after an excruciating silence. "You know I'm kidding, right, Babe?"

"Sure."

"Jaysus, you're sensitive," Hunter teased.

"Sorry," Lydia said hoarsely.

***

The following morning, Lydia awoke with a proverbial chill in her bones.

"Hunter?" she shrieked, sitting bolt upright in bed.

Looking around frantically, Lydia discovered that Hunter was not lying next to her in bed. The morning sun was sneaking through the window while Lydia came to the realization that Hunter was gone. He was supposed to wake her up before he left for Shanghai.

Darting out of bed, Lydia hastily threw on a linty cardigan and flung open the storm door. Outside, Hunter's car was conspicuously absent. All that was left were grooved tired marks in the sandy, dirt driveway.

"Hunter?" Lydia rasped to herself with a single tear escaping her eye.

On the table, exactly where Lydia had placed it alongside Hunter's carryon luggage, was a copy of *Fairweather Friends Forever*. Lydia's lips parted when she realized that despite her best efforts, Hunter had left the book behind.

CHAPTER THIRTEEN

It was pointless to dwell on the dozens of possible reasons Hunter failed to wake Lydia before he left for Shanghai. And yet, Lydia managed to obsess over every single one while floating on an inflatable raft on the lake.

Maybe he did not want to wake her, given the obnoxious hour of his flight.

Maybe he forgot.

Maybe he tried to wake her, but she was sleeping too deeply to be roused.

Maybe he was mad at her for not coming to Shanghai with him.

Maybe he slept through his alarm and had to scramble to get out of the cabin on time.

Maybe Lydia was the last thing on his mind.

Maybe he was so overcome with emotion that he thought it would be too painful to say good-bye.

Maybe he had become so emotionally disconnected from Lydia that it did not occur to him to say good-bye.

Maybe he was chased away by a rogue bear.

Maybe Lydia was overthinking the whole thing.

Hunter would call later.

Sure.

That's it.

He'd call later.

Mesmerized by the water rippling around her raft, Lydia's mind floated to other, more literary things. Inspired by the nature all around her.

"'*For nature gives to every time and season some beauties of its own,*" she mused in her mind. "*And from morning to night, as from the cradle to the grave, is but a succession of changes so gentle and easy, that we can scarcely mark their progress...*' Dickens."

Lydia rolled over on her stomach to catch some rays on her back. As she did so, she noticed her reclusive neighbor outside his cabin. Up closer, she noticed that his eyes were the color of aluminum foil and his nose was distinctly crooked. Lydia furrowed her brow in pensive thought.

"'*In time we hate that which we fear.*' ...Shakespeare."

Lydia shook an unpleasant thought from her head.

***

The canoe wobbled as Lydia found her core balance. She had not been in a canoe since she was seven when she camped in Algonquin Park with her Uncle Sean. She teetered a bit at the start but soon figured out a way to fake it as she paddled around Lovesick Lake, prudently sticking close the shoreline.

Lydia gasped a little when she spotted an otter undulating through the water, sleekly and adorably. She had never seen anything quite so lovable and quirky. A bird of prey swooped overhead – possibly an eagle but more likely a hawk. Lydia would not have known the difference anyway. The sheer wonder of the wilderness around her stoked her imagination in a way that she had never experienced before.

As she passed each boarded-up cottage around Lovesick Lake, she could not help but imagine what secrets were contained inside.

"What do these cabins know?" Lydia thought to herself. *"What stories are hidden underneath all these boards and behind these broken windows? Who once lived there?"*

The first cabin she paddled past was painted blue. Or it had been at one time. Now the paint was chipped, and shingles were flapping in the breeze. A broken tire swing hung sadly from a cedar branch.

"A family of five," Lydia imagined. *"Todd is the dad. The mum is Gale and she is pretty but shy. Three daughters. Two look like Todd. One has a missing tooth. A border collie. Summer retreat. Sounds of laughter, splashing and popcorn popping."*

The second cabin was rotting at the foundation but had good bones. There were wooden shutters on the windows and a sagging spruce loomed above it, offering ample shade.

"Solitary woman," Lydia mused. "Alone by choice. Eyes like glass. Recently purchased a sporty convertible. Two cats. Doesn't need a man. Compensates with binge eating and compulsive suntanning."

The third cabin had a large, sagging porch with three broken steps. A neglected kayak was wedged into what used to be a sand beach but was since overtaken by cattails and fallen logs.

"Newlyweds," Lydia pondered. "Nature buffs. Wool socks and sandals. He likes bass fishing and the left side of the bed. She sits on the dock, knitting pink baby slippers."

And as she drifted by the next cabin, which stood forlorn atop a dramatic rockface cliff...

"Retired Latin professor," Lydia dreamed. "Pipe smoker. Lives with his willowy wife with the polite smile. He cheated. She pretends not to notice. They like to sit for hours in their Adirondack chairs, each sipping a wine cooler."

Before Lydia even realized it, her canoe had drifted closer to the recluse's cabin. She noticed that he was no longer standing outside. She spotted a neglected hatchet stuck in a tree stump, evidence that the hermit had been there recently. Lydia saw a man through the window. He was eating beans directly out of a can with his fingers. Lydia crinkled her nose in disgust. Nonetheless, she tried to get his attention by standing in her canoe, waving her arms around in the air.

"Hello!" Lydia called.

Hearing the commotion, the recluse looked out his window. When he saw Lydia, he quickly closed the curtain.

"Freak," Lydia grumbled.

CHAPTER FOURTEEN

Even after only one day of being in complete seclusion, Lydia was feeling antsy. Although she never would have admitted it. As the sun began to set over the lake like a celestial sorbet, Lydia figured out how to work the barbecue. She grilled a singular hotdog which was looking very lonesome on the grill. Strangely, the silence was starting to embarrass Lydia. She felt the need to fill the silence with the sound of her own voice. Taking advantage of the fact that there was literally nobody around, she made up a little song and made the hotdog dance around by holding it up with tongs.

A random nature sound startled Lydia.

She accidentally dropped the hotdog into the dirt. So much for her very first outdoor culinary adventure.

"Who's there?" Lydia gasped as she spun around.

It was only a woodpecker.

Lydia laughed at herself since nobody was there to laugh at her.

After wiping the dirt from the hotdog with a gingham napkin, (the microbes in the dirt are good for the immune system, yes?) Lydia instinctively set two places at the table. She stopped herself and with an exhale, put the second setting away.

Sitting her bum down on a cushioned, wooden chair and wrapping her mouth hungrily around her hotdog, Lydia's eyeballs lolled over towards the empty chair next to her. Hunter's absence apparently was a presence unto itself. She had eaten alone many times in her Toronto apartment, but this was somehow different. Hunter was farther away this time. And so was Lydia. There was also a conspicuous lack of distractions from Lydia's singularity. And the end game would be in six months and not the usual seven days.

But this was what Lydia wanted, right?

This was Heaven, she reminded herself.

And she would get used to Heaven eventually.

***

Lydia was sound asleep when her cell phone alerted her of an incoming Skype call. She wriggled in her sleep with a perturbed grimace, thinking she was dreaming. Then with a sudden jolt of realization, Lydia's eyes bugged open and she flopped around in her blankets, trying to find her hands. Scrambling, she grappled her phone and answered. A pixelated version of Hunter appeared on the screen.

"Hunter!"

Either an alien responded in a garbled dialect, or Hunter said, *"Babe?"*

"Why are you calling at ridiculous O'Clock?" Lydia rasped, delirious from sleepiness. "You didn't say good-bye even."

Squinting at her phone, the only thing Hunter said that Lydia could decipher as English was, *"time difference."* But that did not answer her question regarding why Hunter left without so much as a hug.

"I miss you," Lydia tried.

"Bad connection..." Hunter said between glitches.

"You forgot the book."

"What?"

"YOU FORGOT THE BOOK."

"Stop yelling at me."

"I'm not... Hunter, I left a copy of my book for you to read on the plane."

"This again... *garble, garble...* No time."

"I saw the recluse today," Lydia tried. "I paddled over. He was eating beans right out of the can."

Hunter's garbles suddenly sounded like they were scolding Lydia.

"I can't hear you, Hunter. Are you mad? You sound like you're mad."

"You went over there?" Hunter barked clearly for the first time. "It's not safe. He doesn't know you're there alone, does he?"

"Calm down, Hunter."

"What if..." Hunter glitched. "... sociopath?"

"I'm fine, Hunter. Nothing happened."

"He had a..." Hunter glitched again. "... had a hatchet."

"Jeez, Hunter. First you leave without telling me. Then after missing you all day you call just to yell at me?"

"Lydia... Lydia..."

"The connection is sketchy. Can I call you tomorrow?"

"No... Conference."

In a huff, Lydia shut off her phone and pulled a wooly blanket over her head.

CHAPTER FIFTEEN

Meredith's Prius was not accustomed to the rugged dirt roads enroute to Elsewhere. She winced each time a rock clanged against the muffler. Patrice sat pertly in the passenger seat, patting Biscotti's head zealously as her eyes penetrated the road ahead. In the backseat was Jules, who was eating seaweed crisps and wishing that she was at a Bjork concert.

"Where are we now, like Timbuktu or something?" Jules complained.

"Can you just stop complaining already?" Meredith seethed. "It was Lydia's choice to move out here. Not mine."

"If she wanted company," Jules sulked, "then she shouldn't have moved somewhere that doesn't even have the good sense to be on a map."

"We are being supportive," Meredith said through clenched teeth. "Lydia is our friend, and we miss her, remember? Because we are good people. *Good people.*"

"We haven't seen Lyds in three weeks," Patrice reminded Jules. "If we don't visit her soon, she'll never stop pestering us."

"And also," Meredith said, raising and index finger, "we are supportive."

"You just want a free vacation," Jules grunted.

"When was the last time you saw a Starbucks?" Patrice asked.

"They don't have Starbucks in the backwoods," Meredith said, rolling her eyes.

"Do they have coffee even?" Patrice moaned.

"How am I supposed to know?"

"Do you even know where we are right now, Mer?" Jules asked.

"This can't be right," Meredith said, consulting Lydia's directions.

"This bumpy road is going to ruin my posture," Patrice pouted.

"Shut up."

"Do you suppose there's a massage therapist around here?"

"Sure, Patrice. Right next to the Starbucks."

"Oh my god!" Patrice shrieked. "Is that a squirrel?"

***

The sound of tires crackling over gravel caused Lydia to cock her head like an inquisitive spaniel. She burst out the door and nearly exploded with glee when she saw a tan Prius come to a tentative stop in front of the cabin.

"Mer!" Lydia squealed, waving cartoonishly.

When Meredith, Patrice and Jules emerged from the car, Lydia scrambled towards them, arms outstretched in a way that could be interpreted as desperate. The girls stood stiffly, surveying their surroundings with revulsion and perhaps fear.

"You made it!" Lydia exhaled breathlessly. "What do you think of the place? Something out of a dream, am I right?"

"If by dream you mean *graphic nightmare*..."

"Jules!" Meredith hissed warningly.

Lydia chewed the side of her cheek when she noticed the girl's city attire. Clearly it had not occurred to them to throw on some jeans, flannels or dirt-worthy footwear. They looked like they were fresh out of *Banana Republic*. Patrice even had the blissful ignorance to wear her fashionably uncomfortable Jimmy Choo heels. That should be fun.

"I'll help you with your..." Lydia trailed off when she noticed Patrice's liberally sized luggage, "...bags."

"Awesome sauce," Patrice said. "The rest is in the trunk."

"Would you like to borrow some hiking boots or..."

"I don't understand the question," Patrice squinted.

Just as Lydia opened her mouth, scrounging for a response, she noticed Meredith and Jules had already headed for the cabin and had begun adjudicating the place. Grabbing an armload of luggage, she trudged down to join them, only to spin right back around when she heard a shrill noise emitting from Patrice's throat. Her stiletto heel had sunk into a boggy mess on the organic, earthen stairs leading down to the cabin.

"Jimmy Choo! Jimmy Choo!" Patrice shrieked with her hands fanning around like a flapping budgie.

"What the..."

"I'm stuck in this vile substance!"

"Dirt?"

"Help me!" Patrice begged, reaching for Lydia like the hysterical heroine in a telenovela. "The mud is swallowing my shoe! It's satanic!"

Unsure of why such a minor wardrobe malfunction had reached this level of emergency, Lydia took Patrice by the forearms and yanked. As Patrice uttered a melodramatic grunt of protest, her dainty, exfoliated foot escaped her shoe, which had now been properly osmosed into the mud.

Lydia shrugged as Patrice's face contorted into a raisin of repugnance.

**

The scintillating aroma of fresh lake bass sizzling in a cast iron skillet wafted through the air. This is what inspired the three identical expressions of utter confusion as Lydia brought dinner to the table. Taking a seat between Meredith and Patrice, Lydia beamed with pride and scoped around the table, looking for signals of approval.

"I caught it this morning," Lydia said in response to the awkward silence in the room.

"Delirium?"

"Fish," Lydia said, forking an equal portion onto each obsolete Melmac dish. "I took the canoe out at around dawn. You should see the sunrises up here. They're like something out of a *Group of Seven* painting. Anyhow, I got this guy on the third cast. He put up quite a fight, but..."

"*He?*" Patrice asked, reviled. "What are you saying? My dinner is gendered?"

"It..." Lydia blinked, "...had to be either one or the other."

"Everything that's alive is gendered," Meredith droned superiorly.

"Untrue," Jules interjected dryly. "Banyans. Banyans are non-gender specific."

"This fish was *alive?*" Patrice gagged.

"How are you this stupid?" Jules squinted.

"I..." Lydia said, genuinely dumbfounded, "... I thought you knew, Patrice. I don't know what to say."

"Nope," Patrice said, pushing her dish away and wagging a finger at it for some reason. "So much nope."

"I'll pass also," Meredith said, in a demure cadence of course.

Lydia gaped, then looked at Jules for validation.

"Would it have killed you to buy some organic hemp loaf?" Jules muttered.

"Organic hemp loaf?" Lydia squeaked with disappointment. "But you said in your text yesterday that you abandoned the flour, meal and grain lifestyle for personal reasons."

"I did," Jules sighed exasperatedly. "Yesterday. That was before I experienced enlightenment."

"But I thought you identified as Icelandic," Lydia said to her friend who was clearly of Irish descent. "So I thought this fresh lake bass would be a treat. Seeing as how Icelandic people eat fish in copious amounts."

"I discovered hemp," Jules said, forcing herself to be tolerant of her oblivious friend. "It changed my life."

"Girl," Meredith asked with an inquisitively curled lip, "when did you discover hemp?"

"It was a long drive," Jules shrugged.

"You became a hemp activist in the car?"

"Don't judge."

"How do you become a hemp activist in a car?"

"I downloaded an app."

"There's an app?"

"There's always an app."

"Even if it was possible to obtain organic hemp products in Elsewhere Township," Lydia added, "how would I even be aware of your lifestyle change when you only jumped on the trend a few hours ago?"

"If you truly knew me," Jules said, slitting her eyes, "I wouldn't have to tell you. And hemp is not a trend. It's a state of being."

Saving herself from her duty to reply, Lydia mashed a forkful of fish into her mouth and chewed it for an awkward amount of time. Mindfully delaying the inevitable, she nodded stupidly at each of her guests, hoping someone would change the subject. Thank God for Meredith's incessant need to control every situation.

"How have you been doing, Lyds?" Meredith said with a voice that literally impaled the silence. "All alone here? In this... shanty? Are you losing your mind?"

"Nope," Lydia nodded. "I have everything I need. And I'm so inspired, you know? This water... I don't have to turn on the faucet anymore. I mean, unless I literally have to turn on the faucet."

Lydia's voice trailed when she noticed Patrice obsessing over her one foot that lacked a shoe. Patrice pouted as she zeroed in on her wiggling toes. She only brought one pair of shoes.

"Do you have any seeds?" Jules asked, hungrily inspecting some rustic cabinets. "Seeds that I can pretend are hemp?"

"Seeds?" Lydia asked, inaudible from defeat.

"You don't have seeds?" Jules grunted with annoyance. "Of any kind?"

Lydia grasped for words.

"Good God," Meredith snapped, "would you just feed the girl before she conforms to the Noom diet?"

"I miss my shoe," Patrice whimpered. "It was so yellow."

"Would the two of you just…" Meredith snapped. "Lydia, how have you been enduring the monotony?"

"I'm fine, Mer. I'm making progress on my book. And… and check out my hands! There's literally no reason to use hand sanitizer out here because of the blatant lack of human germs. My hands aren't chafing anymore. They are so smooth and milky. Go ahead. Feel."

"And you are surviving… how?"

"What do you mean?"

"Food," Meredith said, biting her lower lip a bit too hard while pronouncing the letter F, "clothing, hair products, female hygiene essentials…"

"Birth control," Jules blurted.

"Jules, don't be ignorant," Meredith scolded. "What is she going to do with such thing in the middle of nowhere?"

"Elsewhere," Lydia corrected.

"Don't tell me you subsist by grappling around for lake bass?"

"I have a rod," Lydia remarked, feeling suddenly cornered. "And there's plenty of food at Filbert's."

"Your friend?" Meredith asked, again with that accusatory Letter F.

"General store," Lydia said, finding it difficult to swallow. "They have pretty much everything I need there. Canned goods. Freezer food. Mosquito lanterns. Bait..."

"So other people live here? In this... place?"

"A few," Lydia nodded earnestly. "Although they don't say too much, and they stare which is a little off-putting. But they mean well."

Meredith squinted at Lydia and shook her head disapprovingly.

"I also started growing my own food," Lydia said, trying to distract herself from the speeding of her anxious heart. "I picked up a gardening book at Filbert's and some seeds..."

"Seeds?" Jules asked suspiciously.

"I started a little garden patch outside the cottage. I started with snap peas and radishes," Lydia felt the need to explain, "but I'm getting a bit more adventurous. Heritage Tomatoes. Purple carrots. Edible flowers. Like the ones they put on the ornamental salads? Do you want an ornamental salad? The lettuce at Filbert's is a bit limp and tired but I'm thinking of growing my own so next time you all come..."

"And Hunter? He calls you upon the hour?"

"Not as often as that. There's the time difference and all. But we talk. It's nice. I mean he's in meetings usually and gets a bit short with me because the meetings are important, and I can't just... It's my fault really. I mean... He's tired. Snippy. When tired. Because of the time difference. Did I say that already?... And... and now you guys are here. We're going to have so much fun, you guys. I thought we could take the canoe out tomorrow. Maybe hike down to the gorge. Fish…"

The girls stiffened.

"I get it guys, I do," Lydia sighed. *"Nothing is as painful to the human mind as a great and sudden change'* …Shelley."

"Who's Shelley?"

"Frankenstein," Lydia blinked.

"Shelley is Frankenstein?"

"I was being literary," Lydia explained. "You know. Because I'm… literary?"

"Girl," Meredith said gently, "has the isolation made you fall off your onion?"

"I'm just trying to say," Lydia quavered, unsure of why she was having an anxiety attack in the presence of friends, "that it's understandable you guys might be a little uncomfortable here. At first. But you're going to love it here once we find Patrice's shoe."

"Oh, Hun!" Patrice said, puckering her ridiculous lip cushions. "Mer is right. You've gone batshit. Poor dolly."

"Finally, from so little sleeping," Lydia feebly attempted to joke, *"and so much reading, his brain dried up and he went completely out of his mind.'"*

Blank expressions.

"Cervantes," Lydia tried.

"She's doing it again," Jules stage whispered.

"I'm just trying t…," Lydia said, practically in tears. "Ugh! Eliza used to love it when I implemented literary quotes in casual conversation."

"Eliza?"

"The lady who cleaned the toilets at my former workplace."

"Oh dear God."

CHAPTER SIXTEEN

The next morning, they were gone.

Lydia was expecting to hear the twitter of female voices when she awoke, or perhaps the distinct *klack, thump, clack, thump* of Patrice walking around on the hardwood wearing one shoe. She thought maybe she would smell toast or the fake brew of instant coffee. But instead, she opened her eyes to a familiar stillness in the air that was thicker than margarine.

She discovered a note on the table, pinned under a salt shaker.

"Lyds... Please forgive our ill manners. We wanted to say good-bye, but we had to leave at an obscene hour so as to hit the road early. We literally hate ourselves for leaving basically the same day we arrived, but there was an unforeseeable emergency at my work and since I'm the only one who knows what I'm doing over there, I needed to leave immediately. And it's my car so... Also, I couldn't leave the girls behind seeing as how Pat only had one shoe, and J lacked hemp. Then there's the whole squirrel thing with Patrice. It's clinical and can't be helped. Congrats on your shack. I know artists find filth and poverty utterly poetic, so we are very happy for you. Anyhow, forgive us for being such fussy guests. While we may not have expressed it outwardly, we were smiling in our hearts. We're busy, otherwise we would have LOVED to come back again another time. Kisses!... Mer."

Lydia stared at the note for a solid fifty-three seconds, rereading the third sentence three times to make sure her sleep-crusted eyes were not deceiving her. This was not how she had expected her weekend to go – this *was* the weekend, right? All the days started blurring together, rendering Lydia oblivious to the notion of time.

With a heaving sigh, Lydia nestled on the itchy, tweed couch and texted Hunter.

"They left," was all that Lydia's thumbs, numb with fatigue could manage typing.

Lydia stared at her phone, waiting for the ridiculous talky-dots to start undulating on the screen. When there was no reply after fifteen minutes, she tried again.

"I'm bummed, Hunter. Can we chat?"

Lydia focused on the screen, perhaps trying to will a text to pop up.

"Hunter, are you there?"

Lydia startled when an angry emoji appeared on her phone.

"What's with the angry emoji?" Lydia typed vigorously with perturbation creased on her forehead.

"Are you aware of the time?" Hunter texted back.

Lydia's grimace smoothed as she pondered. Time made no sense anymore.

"Sorry," Lydia typed, biting her lip.

"*I have an important presentation first thing tomorrow.*"

"*I didn't know.*"

"*How could you possibly not know that? It's been the only thing on my mind for the past week and a half.*"

Wait. The *only* thing on his mind?

"*You didn't tell me,*" Lydia typed.

"*What's the big emergency?*"

"*What do you mean?*"

"*You texted me in the middle of the night. I'm assuming this is important.*"

"*I'm lonely.*"

"*Seriously?*"

"*The girls left while I was asleep.*"

"*That's why you texted me?*"

"*I don't think they're coming back.*"

"*Lyds, this is going to have to wait until tomorrow.*"

"*But tomorrow will be the middle of the night.*"

"*This presentation is everything.*"

"*Can we set up a time to talk?*"

No reply.

"Hunter?"

Still no reply.

With her eyes pooling with glistening tears, Lydia curled tightly into a ball.

Alone.

CHAPTER SEVENTEEN

Another two and a half weeks went by, but Lydia was not keeping track. One day just blurred into the next. The silence was beautiful but deafening at times. But this is what Lydia had yearned for.

Solitude.

As per usual, Lydia made herself comfortable at her favorite writing spot; a nest of moss and cedar needles, sheltered by protective tree boughs and hidden in a naturalistic alcove of rock and fallen logs. Her secret lair was shelved upon a flat tier of Canadian Shield, offering a breathtaking view of the lake. The glittery water would mesmerize Lydia, taking her to cloistered depths of her imagination.

The upside to seclusion was the privilege of concentration and productivity. When Lydia squinted at the lake pensively enough, she could almost forget that she was alone. The characters, ideas and concepts that percolated in her brain were more graphic than anything she had ever experienced. Her words flowed freely and effortlessly. Lovesick Lake was the ultimate muse. And every challenge Lydia was facing on her *planet of one* was a thousand times worth it, she decided. Her new novel would be a masterpiece.

It would have been nice to occasionally talk to someone though.

Lydia's focus was suddenly shattered like shards of broken glass when she heard a chattering noise. She discovered a chipmunk at her feet, who stood on his hinds, hoping Lydia would share the bag of peanuts she was munching on. The chipmunk's cuteness caused Lydia to melt into a puddle of sentimental goo.

"Hey, Buddy," Lydia said in a soothing voice. "What's going on?"

The chipmunk chattered adorably.

"Somebody's hungry," Lydia said, dimpling.

Lydia offered the chipmunk a peanut, pinched between her thumb and index finger. The chipmunk gratefully took the nut into his little chipmunk hands and stuffed it into his cheeks. Lydia could not help but laugh heartily at the chipmunk's cuteness.

"Can I call you Rocky?" Lydia said, allowing the chipmunk to taste the salt on her fingertip.

Rocky, as he was now called, crawled into the bag of peanuts and helped himself to the trove. Lydia was gleefully entertained, but then caught a sudden glimpse of the weird recluse across the lake.

"Hey Rocky," Lydia said, not really caring how ridiculous it was to talk to a woodland creature, "you've been here longer than me. What do you know about that old hermit across the lake?"

Rocky was more concerned with the peanuts than he was with Lydia's question.

"I think he's been alone so long he's gotten a little shy. I should be the one to make the first move. What do you think?"

Rocky's eyes bulged at Lydia as his cheeks swelled beyond capacity.

"I agree," Lydia replied playfully. "As cute as you are, and I *do* appreciate your company, I should really find a way to connect with another human. And there's slim pickings around here, eh Rocky? That weirdo may be my only source of companionship until Hunter comes home. Maybe he's not as peculiar as he seems."

***

Dipping her paddle into the glassy water, making drippy ripples, Lydia ventured across the lake with her sights set on the droopy cabin in the distance. As she approached the shore, anxiety twisted her insides like a wet towel being wrung of moisture. Maybe Hunter was justified in warning her against going over there. Was the hermit a psychopath, devoid of conscience, mercy or impulse control? Was he morally insane? A serial killer maybe? Serial killers normally kept to themselves, right? And owned hatchets?

When the tip of her canoe wedged itself into the sandy shore, she rested her paddle diagonally across the yoke and ambled reluctantly towards the neglected shack. She was pretty much committed to the venture at this point, but she flirted with the notion of returning to her cottage to ensure all her limbs would remain intact. She swallowed hard, convincing herself that everything would be okay. He was probably just a lonely old man. Maybe he needed a companion as much as she did.

Lydia rapped on the door.

No answer.

She discreetly peeked in the window that happened to be covered in dead mosquitoes and streaks of bird poop. Through the glass, she spotted the hermit asleep on a couch. Around the room was displayed a disturbing collection of hatchets. Gulping audibly, Lydia reassured herself that this was normal décor in rural places. Aside from the hatchets, she convinced herself, was nothing out of the ordinary, save for the shovel wedged upwards in a conspicuous mound of freshly overturned dirt.

Lydia squeezed her eyes shut.

She gently rapped on the window again.

She whimpered breathily.

The hermit, startled by the window rapping, woke up with a jolt. Then hastily grabbing a hatchet, he darted outside. This was not the reception Lydia was expecting. She dashed cumbersomely back to her canoe, scrambling for the paddle, ugly crying and shrieking involuntarily.

As she paddled hysterically across the lake, panting and flailing, the hermit stood with his hatchet, watching Lydia ominously from the dock.

***

Having locked herself in the cabin for the duration of the day, Lydia made sure every curtain was closed and every light turned off. Her heart was fluttering like a helicopter propellor, so much so that Lydia was convinced she would become airborne. Each time she peeped from behind the curtain, she could see the hermit standing on his dock, staring at her cabin from a distance. Even as dusk settled in and the sky darkened like a slowly swelling ink splotch, he remained on the dock, illuminated by the gas sconces on his porch. Always staring. Never moving. With his hatchet.

Would he ever go back inside?

This was getting freaky.

How long could Lydia realistically remain locked in her cottage?

Lydia noticed a missed phone message on her cell. The message was from a week and a half ago, but having lost her grasp of time, the date held very little meaning to her.

"Beep? What do you mean 'beep?' I hate voicemail. Lyds, it's Hunter. Listen, I didn't mean to snap at you. I realize you're bored but you really need to be a bit more considerate about the time difference, okay? You probably think I'm being a jerk. Blowing off your calls. Look, there's a lot of pressure over here on my end, compounded by the fact that you are so ultra-sensitive… It's hard Lyds. I can't just drop everything… Got another call. Later, Babe."

Hunter.

She *had* to text Hunter.

Lydia's thumbs typed madly on her phone.

"Hunter please answer this time."

No reply.

"Hunter, you can't possibly be asleep now. You're thirteen hours ahead. It's the middle of the night here."

No reply.

"Hunter? Please?"

"Later please. Thnx."

"Hunter, you told me to contact you if there was an emergency. This is an emergency."

"Can it wait?"

"It's an emergency."

"In the middle of presentation..."

"I'm scared."

"Important."

"I saw the recluse."

"Okay, bye."

"He chased me with a hatchet."

"Storytellers..."

"All he does is stare. He's still on the dock now. Staring at me."

No reply.

"What do I do?"

"This is getting embarrassing. Turning my phone off..."

"How can you leave me messages apologizing for blowing me off, and then blow me off when it actually matters?"

No reply.

"Do you even care that I might get julienned and put on a salad?"

No reply.

Lydia shouted a salty word.

After a few lingering moments, her phone rang, displaying an undisclosed number. Muttering Hunter's name, Lydia let it ring. What, was he calling to apologize? Again? Hunter's apologies were starting to mean nothing to Lydia anymore. He became a completely different person since he got his promotion. Emotionally disconnected. Selfish. Married to his job. Brushing her off when she so clearly needed help. How could he be so insensitive to the fact that she was completely isolated while he was hobnobbing in China? Commiserating with real, live humans? Being wined and dined while she ate hotdogs alone? Sometimes raw hotdogs? Nope. Lydia was not answering that phone. Hunter would just have to feel the pangs of rejection, the same as she had.

The phone stopped ringing.

Lydia exhaled.

The phone rang again, this time more antagonistically. Or so Lydia perceived. This was rich. Hunter gave Lydia the cold shoulder because of some elusive presentation and now he was suddenly eager to call her back? Did he suddenly realize how narcissistic he had been of late? Lydia bit her lip.

The phone stopped ringing, but suddenly started again from the same undisclosed number.

Okay this was getting a bit sad. Hunter was clearly contrite. Otherwise, he would not be calling incessantly. Maybe Lydia had judged Hunter too harshly. Perhaps she could have been a little more patient with him, given all his new corporate responsibilities. Industrial plastic can be incredibly stressful, after all. Maybe she had been a bit entitled, calling him and texting whenever she wanted. And she did really need him so...

"Hello?" Lydia said as she quickly answered the phone.

There was no answer.

Only breathing.

"Is anybody there?" Lydia quavered.

"Why didn't you answer the phone?"

"Hunter?"

"No."

"Who is this?"

"You know."

"How did you get this number?"

Heavy breathing.

"How did you get this number?"

Lydia peered out the window, shielding herself with the tweed curtain. She could see a silhouette in the hermit's window. It appeared as though he was looking through binoculars and cradling a cell phone between his cheek and shoulder.

"I can see you," said the voice in the phone. "Nice ducks."

Realizing she was currently wearing pajamas with a quirky duck pattern, Lydia quickly closed the curtain and hid behind the couch. She turned off her phone and dropped it as though it was burning her fingers.

The phone started to ring again. Even more hysterical, Lydia impulsively smashed her cell phone with a meat mallet she hastily grabbed from a cutlery drawer. Then she hurled the cell phone into the blazing fireplace with the charger still inserted like a ridiculous tail. She heaved breathlessly as she watched the phone curl into a melted disfigurement.

No more creepy cell calls.

And also no more phone.

Damn.

Ducking below the window so as not to be seen, she crept into bed, trembling with fear, hiding under her blanket and whimpering.

***

Sleep was out of the question. Lydia remained burrowed under her blanket, her thumping heart the only sound in the troubling darkness. Hunter was right. She never should have engaged with that sinister recluse. She was on his radar now. And here she was in the middle of Elsewhere, a place where nobody could hear her scream. And since she stupidly mutilated her cell phone, she could not even call Hunter for help. Not that he would have taken her seriously.

Lydia could hear the faint sound of a canoe paddle dipping into the still water outside. She could hear boots shlumping through the mud and crunching on the twiggy bramble. Through the sheer curtain, Lydia thought she caught a glimpse of a dark figure approaching the cabin.

Tormented by the approaching noises outside, Lydia tried harder to stifle her terrified whimpers. When the noises seemingly stopped and all was silent, she crept out of bed and lumbered cautiously through the cabin. She pulled the curtain aside to peep outside. The recluse's face was staring emotionlessly at her through the window. Letting out a blood-curdling scream, Lydia threw a cast iron skillet at the window, smashing the glass.

The recluse ducked and shielded himself from the flying, glassy shards before skulking back to his canoe.

Lydia sobbed to the point of exhaustion.

CHAPTER EIGHTEEN

Lydia awoke the next morning to the sound of a slamming car door.

Wait, a car door?

Lydia sat bolt upright in bed, feeling the crust of dried sweat and tears all over her body, hair and clothes.

"Hunter?" Lydia said groggily to no one in particular.

Lydia lurched out of bed, feeling the buzz of exhaustion in her femurs. Pulling on her linty cardigan, she headed outside and looked around to see where the banging and thudding was coming from. She goggled when she saw a jeep parked on the neighboring property. A man was in the process of yanking planks of wood from the boarded-up windows of the cottage next door.

Lydia cocked her head.

Her apparent new neighbor, Lydia could not help but notice, was a rather tanned bloke with a tousled, windswept surfer-style hairdo. His Wrangler jeans fit nicely. And his un-ironed, white t-shirt showcased the conspicuous muscle fibers that quivered each time he wrenched a wood plank off his cottage. Grunting from the effort, the strangely intriguing man stopped briefly to catch his breath, wiping the sweat from his suntanned brow with a sinewy forearm.

Before Lydia knew what was happening, the man took out a bottle of water, tilted his head backwards and took manly swigs, causing his Adam's apple to undulate in a way that made Lydia blush. His loose curls glistened in the sunlight and just sort of fell back into place when his head returned to the upright position. Lydia experienced mild flu-like symptoms when he ran his rugged fingers through his organically unkept locks.

When *What's-His-Name* turned his head towards her, Lydia suddenly realized that she was staring. She stopped breathing for a solid five seconds when his face radiated with a warm smile.

"Oh! Hello!" he said, waving good-naturedly.

Lydia felt her stomach tangle into a pretzel.

She gaped.

"Didn't realize anyone was here," the rural surfer said. He had a deep rasp in his voice as though he routinely gargled with boiling water. He could have been a bluesy bar singer if he was so inclined.

Lydia's mouth moved around but no words emerged.

"A rare treat," he smiled, his eyeballs involuntarily lolling up and down Lydia, which surprisingly, she did not find creepy at all.

Lydia closed her linty cardigan tightly around herself for some reason.

After an awkward pause...

"Are you going to come over here and give me hand or what?" the man dimpled coyly.

But Lydia's feet were apparently stapled to the ground. Her entire body was proverbially paralyzed with awkwardness.

"Don't say much, eh? That's okay, Darlin'. Your terms."

Darlin'? Not only was this guy smolderingly handsome, but also endearing. Like a kind of rural Freddie Mercury.

Lydia croaked out her name, but it sounded more like a spring peeper frog. She silently cussed herself as the dreamy neighbor cocked his head like a confused spaniel. Why did her social anxiety have to betray her now? Not only was this guy a total snog muffin – not that this was relevant to Lydia of course, but still noteworthy – but he was the first living, breathing soul she had encountered in weeks. She could *not* flub her only opportunity to interact with another human. The isolation was really starting to get to her. And she would feel a thousand times safer with a male companion, what with the deranged recluse on her scent.

Come, ON, Lydia! Just blurt something out. Anything! Just...

"I'm," Lydia blurted stupidly.

"I'm?"

"Lydia."

"Lydia?"

Lydia nodded like a petrified pine marten. That nods.

"Granger," the swoony stranger said, extending a hand.

Lydia coughed up a furball.

Granger dimpled reassuringly.

"Seems we're neighbors," he said as Lydia could literally *hear* the smile in his voice.

"Right," Lydia stuttered, hating herself for stuttering. "Sorry... I... I didn't sleep well."

Granger's eyes softened with compassion.

"Plus I've been alone for a while so..." Lydia felt the need to explain.

"You're alone?" Granger asked, triangulating an eyebrow.

Gaping, Lydia ran her thumb over her naked ring finger.

She should say something.

Why couldn't she say something?

"Any good at prying planks off of windows?" Granger winked. "Or would that splinter your smooth little model hands?"

Lydia blinked.

***

"Thanks for the help, Darlin'," Granger said in mid-grunt as he dropped a box of casual dishware on the kitchen floor just inside his cabin. "You okay with that box?"

The cardboard box Lydia was dragging towards Granger's neglected cabin felt like it was filled with river rocks. Lydia stopped when she reached the porch. She was not about to go into a strange man's cabin upon their first encounter, no matter how swoony he was. Or how uplifting his vibrations. Or how strangely drawn she was to him, like a magnet to a refrigerator.

She tentatively peeped through the door of Granger's lonesome shack, which Lydia had imagined once being inhabited by a morose, French immigrant named Thibald – or Gaspard. Lydia waffled between the two. Inside, she saw no angry splotches of French expressionism on the walls, as per the imaginary Frenchman's taste. The window seat lacked a bereted poet-type, glaring glassily out at the lake with a cigarette nestled in his fingers. And there were zero cats wandering around. Thibald, or Gaspard if you prefer, had six cats, who like their refined human, padded elegantly and aloofly around the cabin. With their eyes nothing more than glowing slits in the darkness.

But this cabin and the sun-kissed heartthrob which it contained were freakishly different than anything Lydia had imagined.

From the safety of the porch, Lydia noticed Granger wiggle his nose from the swirling dust that was lingering in the air of the cottage, offering the room a kind of ethereal vibe. She noticed from her brief peep that the room was dank and had a wooden smell like the inside of a cedar chest full of mothballs. And she was pretty sure she heard a squirrel who was trying to scratch its way out from inside a wall. Cobwebs glimmered from the light as Granger ignited a single lightbulb by pulling a chain on the low ceiling. He blinked from the disturbed, airborne dust and sudden illumination in the room.

"Electricity's still on," Granger nodded approvingly. "So there's that."

"Here's your box," Lydia managed to cough.

"If you don't mind dragging it on inside..."

Lydia's lips parted.

"Everything okay?" Granger asked, tilting his head.

Nope. The porch was as far as Lydia would dare go. What did she really know about Granger, exactly? Aside from the fact that his Wranglers hugged his butt superlatively or that his eyes happened to be the same color as her favorite dessert garnish? He also smelled vaguely of campfire smoke and coconut sunscreen, of which Lydia fervently approved. And the first time he smiled at her Lydia basically had an asthma attack. But other than that, she knew nothing about him. Did he have a criminal record? A personality disorder? A woman in the cabin somewhere, being held against her will? An illicit glue habit? A collection of creepy dolls?

"I'll just drag it to the door, how about?" Lydia stuttered. "Then you can... I don't know. Put it wherever you want."

As Lydia yanked the cardboard box it tore, revealing a trove of musty-smelling books inside: Victor Hugo, Oscar Wilde, Charles Dickens, PG Wodehouse, Leo Tolstoy, Christopher Marlowe, Ovid, William Blake, Alfred Lord Tennyson, Edgar Allan Poe... Lydia's eyes glossed with wonder. She did not mean to stare but she could not help it.

'Oh my God, he READS.'

'I mean, he couldn't be all that bad then.'

"I figured I'd be all alone out here," Granger continued, startling Lydia out of her stupor.

"Surprise," Lydia laughed nervously. It was more of an anemic twitter than a laugh though.

"What a strange feeling to be back," Granger said, squinting nostalgically at Lovesick Lake. "Without all the laughter and splashes echoing off the water. Friends waving from their docks. That ridiculous golden retriever paddling after that ball that was bigger than his damn head. Ha!... Shame though. The lake is a husk of what it once was, that's for sure."

"You know this lake then?" Lydia said, running her finger down an Alexander Dumas hardcover.

"This cabin was my vacation home before everyone left."

"Why did you come back?"

"Got the cabin in the divorce settlement," Granger explained, squatting on the porch step with a soda can and inviting Lydia to sit next to him. "Claudia got the bungalow in Gatineau. Also the whippets which makes literally no sense. She doesn't even like dogs. You can deduce for yourself what you think her intentions were with that. But I got the cottage and the Jeep which will do for now. How about you?"

Lydia bristled with nerves.

"How long have you been in Cabin 6?"

"A few weeks," Lydia murmured, averting eye contact. "Or months. I don't know offhand."

"Easy to lose track of time up here, isn't it?" Granger nodded "You've been alone here for weeks? Months? Without anyone to talk to?"

Lydia shrugged.

"You doing okay out here?" Granger nudged. "On your own?"

Lydia's lips parted.

"I don't mean to suggest you need a man to swoop in and interfere," Granger said, scratching his abs in a way that Lydia found distracting. "It's just that you give off a distinct urban vibe..."

"What, do I smell like exhaust fumes? Street food? Pot?"

"Just a vibe," Granger shrugged. "If you need anything..."

"I'm okay," Lydia said quickly.

"Look, I'm here now so if at any point in time you feel unsafe..."

"Why would I feel..."

"Just being alone and all..."

"Is there a reason I should feel unsafe?"

"I just thought it must be a big shift moving here from the city. Eerie calm. Weird noises. Thick, pounding silence. It can play games with your mind if you let it."

"Okay," Lydia blinked hard.

"I'm here, is all I'm saying, Lydia. Just a stone-throw away. It could be good for both of us. I'd be lying if I said I wasn't dreading the monotony of my own company…"

"I just met you though…"

"Right," Granger blinked. "Okay, yes. That is true. And I'm not trying to be imposing. I mean, here you are. Alone in a cabin then all of a sudden a queer man shows up…"

"Oh!" Lydia said, sagging with disappointment. "I didn't realize… I mean not that it matters to me what your preferences are…"

"What…. No!" Granger laughed. "Not queer as in… I'm definitely not into… Odd. I'm odd."

"Odd?"

"Not in a bad way," Granger chuckled. "Just a little quirky in my habits. And looks."

Lydia blinked.

"Claudia often complained that I'm oddly proportioned."

"I disagree," Lydia blurted.

Granger tilted his head thoughtfully.

"I mean…" Lydia stammered, unable to swallow. "You are quite symmetrical. Like a triangle. With the shoulders that do that albatross thing…"

"Albatross?"

"Like the wings," Lydia said, stumbling into an even deeper pit of awkwardness. "Span. The span of the wings. But shoulders. Then you kind of geometrically angle into a…"

"Triangle…"

"Excuse me," Lydia panted, scrambling.

Granger sheltered an amused grin with his hand at the same moment that Lydia flew off the porch step, flailing like a promotional, air-dancing balloon person blowing around at a car dealership.

CHAPTER NINETEEN

Dammit, dammit, dammit, dammit.

Lydia winced when she caught a glimpse of herself in the cracked bedroom mirror. How could she have introduced herself to that suntanned smoke show next door looking like a sleep-deprived wet hamster? She was completely encrusted in dried snot, tears and eye-crispies. Her eyes were swollen into two tired marshmallows with bloodshot slits. And holy crap! Did she actually say those things to him? *With her mouth?*

Flopping on the squeaky bed with an audible whimper, Lydia squeezed her eyes shut, focusing on not focusing on Granger's sexy triangularity. And hair. Eeep! The hair! And his eyes were the color of what, caramel? How was that even fair? Guilt swirled through her body like a lollipop of shame.

"No, no, no, no, no," Lydia moaned, curling in a ball, perhaps to smother her screaming uterus. "You're married, Lydia. Triangles hold no relevance. Why did I have to start blathering on about triangles? Who does that?"

And now she was talking to herself. What a hot steamy mess she was, scrunched in a ball on her bulbous mattress like a blanketed nugget of disgrace. Her temples throbbed with guilt. She had not technically cheated on Hunter. Nope. She had done zero things wrong. At least in terms of literal actions. But she had not crushed so hard on another guy since her pre-Hunter dose of

Trevor. And he was never a real option due to his religious parents and the Munster cheese. (Don't ask) Besides, Trevor was only marginally aware of Lydia's existence since she was the mousiest girl in the whole Post-Colonial poetry club. But Granger had clearly been flirting with his lolling eyeballs and his astute observation regarding the size and texture of Lydia's *model hands.*

Had she flirted back? Lydia felt woozy trying to rewind every frame of her encounter with Granger. In all her awkwardness did she blurt out some kind of kinky innuendo? Did she give off a nuance? Did she look at him weird? At any point in time were her eyes facing the general vicinity of his impressively compact butt? For the luvva... if she was aware of the impressive compactness of his butt then clearly this misdemeanor had already taken place!

Lydia screamed into her pillow.

CHAPTER TWENTY

Sitting on a needly nest in her rocky alcove the next morning, Lydia tapped her pen compulsively on a pad of paper, squinting at the lake in an intense focus. A familiar chatter interrupted Lydia's unproductive trance.

"Rocky!" Lydia bubbled, cupping her hand for the chipmunk to nestle into. "How are things?"

Chatter, chatter, chee, chee, chee.

"I know, right?" Lydia answered as though she was having a literal conversation with the rodent. "Did you um… notice the Jeep over there? And the dude?"

Chit, chit, chit, chit, chitter.

"Yes, Rocky. I noticed too. How could I not notice how yummy… I'm a terrible person, aren't I?"

Rocky obliviously angled for a peanut.

"What about Hunter though? I mean sure, he's been emotionally drifting from me lately… and Granger seems so attentive and considerate…"

Lydia suddenly shook the nasties from her head.

"I'm just lonely, right? I just miss Hunter. And physical contact. I mean, anyone could have shown up in a Jeep – a gaggle of zitty frat boys, a rotund Lithuanian undertaker, a gnarly crone with a sketchy essential oil business, literally anyone named Beauregard, the world's least convincing Elvis impersonator... I would have been fizzing with endorphins no matter who moved in next door. I am most definitely not falling for this guy. I just need some time to cool off. Right? Answer me, Rocky. Am I right?"

Rocky's eyes bulged.

"So what's the right thing to do then? Ignore him? Be aloof? Every member of my body is literally inflamed from isolation. That's a thing you know, Rocky. Isolation can cause inflammation. Not to mention chronic pain, cardiovascular disease, immune deficiency, cytokine storms. I read about it online before I incinerated my cell phone. Everything's inflamed right now, Rocky. My gums. My eyelids. My jaw. My elbows. I really don't know what's going on with my elbows right now..."

Chatter chee?

"I mean I know I wanted seclusion. This is literally what I've always dreamed of. But I'm human, dammit. I crave friendship too. I can't deny myself the inherent right to be human. And Granger seems so nice..."

Rocky shoved a peanut into his cheek.

"And if the recluse comes back... Is it so wrong of me to feel safer with a dude next door? Hunter would want me to feel safe, right?"

Lydia abruptly cocked her head when she heard the crunch of cedar needles underfoot. Peeping over her rocky alcove, she spotted Granger ambling down to his dock.

"There he is, Rocky," Lydia stage whispered. "What do I do?"

No reply.

"I should go down there," Lydia nodded. "Granger is literally the only person I can talk to."

Oblivious, Rocky opened his mouth seemingly wider than his head, but refrained from biting into his peanut when he was suddenly reprimanded by Lydia, unprovoked.

"Don't judge me, Rocky. You would do the same thing if you were in my shoes. And before you say anything, no. I am not being naïve by blindly trusting a man I met yesterday. I'm good at reading auras. And his is beautiful. Platonically beautiful, I should add. And it feels good to be around him. Moderately good. The appropriate amount of good."

Rocky scratched his itchy head with his foot.

"Here I go then," Lydia exhaled. "Don't try to stop me, Rocky. I've made up my mind. Here I... go."

Lydia's knees buckled a little when she stood. Then taking a deep breath and placing a stray strand of hair behind her ear, she tentatively made her way towards the dock upon which stood Granger. He had his hands on his hips and was testing the wooden slats with a thump of his heel.

The splintery dock creaked beneath Lydia's sandaled feet, causing Granger to turn to her with a smile that glowed with amiability.

"Well hi!" Granger said with genuine ardor.

"Hey," Lydia hiccupped, twirling her hair which was mousier and limper than her social skills in that moment.

"Thought I'd see how my dock was holding up," Granger explained, scratching the back of his hair which was curling from sweat. "It's rotting. Barely able to support the two of us standing here. It's a wonder we don't both go crashing right through."

"Oh," Lydia said, quickly retracting from the dock. "I didn't know."

"Hey, no harm done," Granger said, producing a dimple. "I'll get 'er fixed once I pick up some supplies from Filbert's."

After testing the sturdiness of the dock with an intentional wobble, he hopped off the dock and approached Lydia who was now sitting uncertainly on a mossy rock.

"I called you a triangle," Lydia swallowed apologetically.

"You did," Granger stated, scootching his bum next to Lydia on the rock.

"Which was weird."

"I liked it."

"You did?"

"Nobody's ever called me a triangle before."

"I don't really know why I came over here, actually..." Lydia said hastily while poising to dart away like a skittish anole.

"I was hoping you'd come over," Granger said, extending a beckoning hand.

"You were?"

"We're neighbors, after all. I've always made a point to be on good terms with my neighbors. Never know when you might need to borrow a cup of sugar," Granger winked.

The sock of awkwardness expanded in Lydia's mouth, making her tongue dry up.

"What were you doing over there anyhow?" Granger asked while yanking a shrub-sized weed out of the ground by the roots. "In your little nest?"

Lydia swallowed hard. Did Granger hear her talking to a chipmunk? Humiliation bubbled up inside her like uncontrollable magma.

"Working," Lydia said very quickly, hoping if she squeezed her eyes shut, Granger would not notice her rapidly reddening cheeks.

"What is it that you do?"

"Things," Lydia nodded stupidly. "I write them."

Granger's eyes glowed dreamily like a cat falling asleep.

"That's what I do, I mean," Lydia said, wincing.

"A writer," Granger said, evaluating Lydia's boho tunic with a fresh fondness. "Are you productive out here?" Granger asked, genuinely curious. "Is it inspiring with all this glorious, glassy water?"

Lydia's eyes bulged with surprise.

Someone else was aware of water's mystical influence?

Someone cared about her productivity?

Someone... cared?

"To be honest," Lydia said after clearing away some nervous phlegm, "I was super-productive when I first arrived. But lately..."

Granger nodded earnestly, hanging on her every word.

"I..." Lydia stammered, "... it's a little hard to be truly inspired with literally nobody around."

Granger squinted across the lake, shielding his eyes from the sun.

"Looks like we're not entirely alone," he droned.

When Lydia followed Granger's glance across the lake, she gasped a little when she saw the strange hermit standing on his dock, staring at them from afar.

"He's still here, is he?" Granger rasped.

"Do you know who he is?" Lydia asked with widening eyes.

"The deranged nut loaf with the hatchets?" Granger said through clenched teeth. "He's a recluse. He's been living here longer than anyone can remember. Refused to leave so everyone else did."

"I thought everyone left because of property taxes."

"Is that what they told you?" Granger asked, quirking an eyebrow.

"Is... he dangerous?"

"Hard to say," Granger replied. "When you've been alone as long as he has, you sort of get stuck inside your own mind. It got worse with time, I noticed. His episodes. Maybe if he integrated into our little community, he wouldn't have spiraled the way he did. But the weird ones like to keep to themselves, don't they? The best thing you can do is stay out of his way. It's doubtful that he'll adapt to change very well."

Lydia's lips parted as she stared at the recluse with a faint tremor in her breath.

Granger noticed.

"You didn't go over there…" Granger said in a slightly deeper voice.

"I… yes."

Granger's forehead creased with a maze of worry for a moment, but wiped the look of concern from his face with a swipe of his hand.

"It can't be helped now," he sighed. "Don't worry, Darlin'. We'll look out for each other. I know his ways."

Lydia visibly stiffened with apprehension.

"It'll be okay," Granger said as he put a reassuring hand on Lydia's shoulder. "He won't bother you as long as I'm around. He knows I don't take his guff."

Normally Lydia would flinch if someone – especially a stranger would unexpectedly touch her. But surprisingly, when she felt Granger's hand on her shoulder blade, she melted into a kind of buttery calm. Like there was a pleasant, fuzzy vibration emitting from his palm into her soul. She closed her eyes for a moment and savored it.

"Lydia?"

"Hmm?"

"You drifted."

"Sorry."

"The nut loaf is still watching us."

"He..."

"What do you say the two of us get out of here?"

"In what sense?"

"I need a few things from Filbert's," Granger said, pursing his lips hopefully. "Want to come with?"

***

Lydia sat woodenly in the passenger seat of Granger's Jeep, her posture ridiculously rigid, her hands cupped genteelly in her lap and her eyes bugging out of the sockets as she goggled out the front windshield. She flinched as Granger hopped into the driver's seat and shut the car door.

"Ready?" Granger asked, nestling his butt into a comfortable position and curling his fingers around the steering wheel.

What was she doing in some dude's Jeep? Sure, Granger had a comforting spirit that Lydia found addictive. Whenever he was around, she felt like her soul was reposing in a warm, soothing bubble bath. Deep down she knew that Granger had a gentle heart and would never do anything to hurt her. But he was still a new person. And a man. With quivering muscles. And specific knowledge that she was alone on an abandoned lake. This was plausibly the most irresponsible thing she had done since she was three and attempted to breach the spider monkey exhibit at the Toronto Zoo. Lydia liked spider monkeys.

"Lydia?" Granger asked empathetically when he noticed Lydia stiffening into a pillar of salt of Biblical proportions.

"I like spider monkeys," Lydia blurted stiffly.

"You okay?"

"Yes," Lydia said, shaking her head.

Granger relaxed his fingers from the steering wheel and pursed his lips. He subtly nodded to himself, then ignited his face with a smile. "What do you say we walk to Filbert's?"

Lydia slowly softened like a boiling noodle.

"Be a shame to miss out on all this sunshine," he winked.

The corner of Lydia's mouth curled into a smile as she put her little hand into Granger's and hopped out of the Jeep. The brief contact caused a tiny electrical current to twinge through her skin and course through her entire body. Or maybe it was just static. She adjusted her slouchy peony hat as they ambled up the graveled driveway toward the deserted street ahead. She ran out of moisturizing conditioner a few days ago so her hair was stringier and limper than usual. And she felt a niggling need to look pretty for the first time in weeks. Hence, the hat.

"Nice hat," Granger tried.

"Are you being sarcastic or..."

"I just like hats."

"Oh... thank you."

"I respect a girl who can wear a hat."

"You do?"

"It's bold."

"Bold?"

"Not every woman can pull it off. The way I see it, every woman secretly wants to wear a hat, but most are too afraid it won't suit them. Like they think their head needs to be a certain shape, I don't know. And those who are too modest to try one on, which is nearly all of them, will never know. It's sad if you think too hard about it."

Lydia's eyeballs lolled upwards towards the slouchy brim. "I wouldn't really describe myself as bold."

"You need to be kinder to yourself, Darlin'."

"Sorry."

"For what?"

"I'm awkward around new people."

"Nothing to apologize for."

"I get anxious sometimes. It can be annoying. To me and those around me."

"That why you left the city?"

"Unreal City, I had not thought death had undone so many. Sighs, short and infrequent, and each man fixed his eyes before his feet..."

"...Eliot."

"...Yes," Lydia blinked. "How did you..."

"Not much of a city guy myself. I spent three days in Ottawa and it nearly ended me. Too impersonal for my taste. City dwellers are so disconnected. Just walking around, completely unaware of anyone else. I once read that's what Hell is like."

"Hell is other people..."

"... Sartre," Granger winked.

Lydia's eyes flared.

"See," Granger continued, "it can get lonely out here, but consider the trees. More trees than people out here, and they don't shut people out. It's like they're communicating with us. With their energy. Their stillness. Their sway. Tells you a lot when the trees can communicate better than humans who speak with literal grammar and syntax."

Lydia gaped at Granger with her lips parted.

"Told you I was odd," Granger said, playfully elbowing Lydia.

"I used to have a friend," Lydia gulped, "who bantered with me using literary quotes."

"Sounds like a fun gal."

"She was."

Lydia exhaled like a contented balloon when Granger put his hand on the small of her back, guiding her up a hill in the road.

CHAPTER TWENTY-ONE

The aisles were narrow at Filbert's General Store. As Lydia was perusing the selection of instant noodles on a slanted shelf, Granger hovered nearby. There was barely enough room for both of them to squeeze between the shelves of campy food, so more than once Lydia felt Granger's firm body brush up against hers. Normally, Lydia would feel claustrophobic in such a context, but this time Lydia relished the warmth of Granger's essence.

"Do you see any canned meatball stew?" Granger asked as Lydia felt this soothing breath on the back of her neck. "I need to pick something up for dinner."

"Found it," Lydia proclaimed as she popped a can into a half-sized grocery cart.

"Maybe grab two of those," Granger said, slapping his back pocket. "Damn."

"What's up, Granger?"

"Well, this is embarrassing," Granger said, sliding his fingers through his hair. "Forgot my wallet."

"I can take care of it," Lydia smiled cutely.

"I can't let you do that, Darlin'."

"I don't mind."

"This must look bad."

"Granger, no. You obviously didn't forget your wallet on purpose."

"You forget what you want to remember, and you remember what you want to forget..."

"... McCarthy," Lydia smiled coyly.

Granger produced a pair of enamored dimples. "You're good at this game."

"Grab anything you want," Lydia offered. "It's on me."

"Darlin'..."

"It's my way of welcoming you back to Elsewhere."

"I will reimburse you as soon as we get back to the cottages."

"No need."

"I insist though. I..."

During an awkward maneuver, Lydia and Granger got wedged together, seemingly conjoined by their torsos when they tried to turn a crammed corner.

"Excuse me..." Lydia blushed.

"Excuse *me,*" Granger said breezily, locking eyes with Lydia for a moment.

"Um..." Lydia said nervously, "...people are looking."

"Right," Granger said, wriggling free.

The grocery cart squeaked like a verbose rat as Lydia brisk-walked towards the cashier. "We should get out of here. Long walk home."

"Sure," Granger said, following Lydia and plunking a few more personal items into the cart.

A shaggy-eyebrowed cashier greeted Lydia with nothing more than a suspicious glare. He said nothing as he scanned the items in Lydia's cart.

"Hey there," Lydia said shyly, averting eye contact.

The cashier, who's nametag admitted his name was Henrik, simply stared at her.

"Don't let him bother you," Granger said breezily into Lydia's ear. "People around here are wary of outsiders. They stare a lot. That's just their way."

"He's creeping me out."

"I know. Just try not to let it bother you."

Henrik picked up a pair of men's underpants and glared at Lydia quizzically.

"They're his," Lydia felt the need to explain, while pointing at Granger with her thumbs.

Granger had drifted over to the wilderness aisle and was examining a can of insect repellent. Henrick craned his neck towards Granger, glared at him for a bit and shook his head in annoyance, muttering something unintelligible while scanning Granger's stew, whey protein and lumberjack-strength deodorant.

"Don't give the girl a hard time," Granger called over to Henrik. "She's doing me a solid, so just mind your own beeswax."

Henrik rolled his eyes from under his jungle of eyebrows.

"The man needs underpants," Lydia said, pursing her lips in perturbance. "Stop judging. Jeez."

"Sorry," Granger said, catching up with Lydia and putting an apologetic hand on her shoulder. "I really should have waited until next time to pick up the personal items. I didn't mean to embarrass you like that."

"Did you see the way that guy looked at me?"

"Yes," Granger said, ushering Lydia out of the store. "They are ultra-rural out here. They have nothing else to do but form opinions about people's purchases. Then someone new comes along and it just about blows their minds. Remember, there's only like twenty-five permanent residents out here and it's not exactly a touristy area. They are not used to outsiders. Seeing a new person is quite an ordeal for them."

"He didn't even say anything to me," Lydia said as they began their hike up the gravel road. "Not a single word."

"You get used to it," Granger said, chivalrously taking the grocery bags from Lydia's clutches.

"Am I going to be like that after a few years in Elsewhere?" Lydia shuddered.

"Not if you stay connected," Granger winked. "Guess it's a good thing we found each other."

"It is a great misfortune to be alone, my friends; and it must be..."

"...believed that solitude can quickly destroy reason."

Lydia and Granger said the word *'Verne'* at the same time as they serendipitously locked eyes.

Reddening, Lydia looked away.

***

A sagging feeling of disappointment consumed Lydia when she spotted the cottages up ahead through a grove of cedars. The walk home with Granger did not seem like a two hour walk and she was strangely saddened by the end of the journey. That obnoxious number six was taunting her on the cottage door, reminding her that the most natural, fluid conversation she had ever had with another person was winding down. They had talked about books, characters, archetypes, tropes and even drifted into a tangent about empaths, interconnectedness and the baseness of the human condition.

"So erm..."

"Yep..."

There was an all-encompassing silence that made Lydia feel as though someone was sitting on her chest. Perhaps a silverback gorilla.

"I mean," Granger tried, "I did get the two cans of stew. Or rather, you did."

"What?"

"There's no point in us eating dinner separately."

Lydia's lips parted.

"This," Granger said, running his hand through his wavy locks, "is my cumbersome way of inviting you over for dinner."

"... Oh."

Please don't run away, screaming. Please don't run away, screaming. Please don't run away, screaming.

The good news is, Lydia managed to suppress her screams and only did so in her mind as she ran flailing into her cabin, leaving Granger blinking blankly at Cabin 6.

CHAPTER TWENTY-TWO

Something felt different when Lydia's eyelids fluttered open the following morning. The bed felt warmer somehow. Her nostrils became aware of a comforting aroma that had absorbed into her sheets – coconut and campfire smoke?

With a gasp, she sat bolt upright in bed.

"Morning, Darlin'," Granger said dotingly with his eyebrow quirking with innuendo.

"WHOA!" Lydia squawked, frantically gathering sheets around herself. "What the actual…"

"Sleep well?"

"Granger, what are you doing in my bed?"

"I was watching you sleep up until a second ago. So adorable the way you coo like a little pigeon each time you stir in your blankets."

"What's going on?" Lydia asked, hugging her knees for emotional support. "Did we…"

"Snuggle? Oh yes."

"Wait, what? We snuggled?"

"Yep."

"Why?"

"Because you wanted to snuggle."

Lydia squinted and shook her head interrogatively.

"The look on your face implies that you may have consumed a little too much whiskey last night."

"I don't drink whiskey," Lydia spat, squeezing her eyes shut.

"That's what you said when I brought some over," Granger nodded. "But you didn't want to be rude so..."

"Why did you bring whiskey over?"

"You don't remember any of it?"

Lydia's eyes widened and twitched.

"Take it easy, Darlin'. All that happened was... you called me over when you heard noises outside. You thought it was the nut loaf lurching around or something, I don't know. You wanted me to sit with you a while. I brought beverages because I figured it would be gentlemanly to do so, seeing as how I was a guest in your home. It got late. You invited me to stay and..."

"Snuggle?"

"You were scared."

"I don't invite guys to stay and snuggle."

"Does that mean I'm special?"

"Oh my God, oh, my God, oh my God, oh my God," Lydia lamented, curling tightly into a ball, hiding her face in shame.

"Lydia..." Granger said soothingly, sliding closer to her.

"Do I even have pants on? I can't look."

"You do."

"Did we..."

"We just snuggled."

"Did I like it?" Lydia winced.

"Oh yes."

"I think I might throw up."

"You did ingest a lot of whiskey for a little person."

"Granger," Lydia cringed. "There is something I should tell you. I have a... I mean I'm ma..."

Granger took Lydia's chin and tilted her head to face him. "Can I kiss you first?"

"That would be pleasant, but the thing is, Granger, wait..."

As Granger leaned in gingerly with his lips puckered into what looked like a perfect, plush rosebud, Lydia suddenly heard someone singing what was probably a regional folk song. Cocking her ear, she determined that the voice most definitely belonged to Granger. Her brow furrowed quizzically as she zeroed in on Granger's puckering lips.

"Granger? How is it possible that you are singing and puckering at exactly the same moment?"

"I'm kind of busy here."

"And now you are talking. While singing. How is this a thing?"

"I don't hear anything."

"You don't hear yourself singing?"

"Damn, Girl. Would you just shut your gob and kiss me already?"

Lydia stiffened when Granger ravished her unexpectedly, causing them both to fumble onto the floor.

The thud from Lydia falling out of bed, not to mention her throbbing tailbone, caused her to suddenly wake up. Gasping, Lydia frantically scoured the room, but Granger was not there. And the room no longer smelled like coconut and campfire smoke. However, she could still hear Granger singing in his deep, raspy voice. She followed the sound outside where she found Granger repairing her kitchen window. He stopped singing in mid-lyric when he spotted Lydia standing on the porch, stupefied. He shook the sweat from his hair like a wet dog.

And he wasn't wearing a shirt.

Rapidly reddening, Lydia turned away and focused on an atypical fungus growing out of the side of a tree trunk.

"Did I wake you?" Granger asked.

"It's all good," Lydia said, waving in Granger's general direction while still staring at the fungus.

"Hope you don't mind," Granger said, climbing down from a step ladder. "I noticed your window was smashed. Everything okay?"

"I'm good," Lydia said, still averting eye contact, still waving. "Everything's good."

"But your window was smashed."

"It was an accident. Cast iron skillet."

"Through the window?"

"Happens."

"Are you sure you're okay?"

"Fine."

"Is this about me inviting you to dinner or..."

"No!"

"Because you kind of ran away. Flailing."

"I do that sometimes."

"Did I overstep? Coming over here to fix your window? Because I didn't mean..."

"I just had a confusing dream and it's shaking me up a bit."

"Sounds graphic."

"Extremely."

"You know, being alone too long can affect your dreams."

"I don't really want to talk about it."

"Must have been some dream," Granger said, taking the liberty to steady Lydia's quaking hand for a moment.

"It just seemed so real."

"You're safe now, Darlin'. You know that, right?"

Lydia nodded. Granger's presence did indeed feel stabilizing.

"You sure you don't want to talk about it?" Granger asked, cocking his head. "Might help."

"No!" Lydia said much too quickly.

Granger's eyes flared with sudden realization, causing him to instantly redden. "... Oh... I should go..."

"I didn't specifically say that the dream was about you..." Lydia blurted, instantly wincing afterwards. "I mean..."

"I know what you mean... I'll just... Bye."

"Granger, wait! It's not what you think!"

Lydia suddenly felt like digging a hole to crawl into. A hole that was deeper, bleaker and more claustrophobic than the metaphorical one she already fell into.

CHAPTER TWENTY-THREE

"I am such an idiot," Lydia fretted privately to Rocky in the privacy of her alcove. "Now Granger knows I had an almost-dirty dream about him which is totally going to ruin everything. I have to find the right balance, you know? Find a way to absorb his soothing anima without being a literal strumpet. It just feels so natural to be around Granger. This is the most alive I've felt in weeks, Rocky. But I have to keep things neutral. If things go too far..."

Chuck, chuck, chuck, chitter.

"I've been trying to resist the urge to flirt with the guy, but let's keep it real. When a guy walks around looking like *that,* flirting is basically an involuntary spasm and completely outside of my control. I mean on that walk home from Filbert's I flirtatiously flipped my hair. Can you *even,* Rocky? I never flip my hair. Who knew I could be so brazen?"

Chit, chit, chuck, chuck, chuck.

"It's not my fault, Rocky. How can I be expected to control myself with Granger's irresistible odyl?"

"My odyl?" Granger said, pursing his lips to suppress a giggle.

"Jaysus!" Lydia shrieked when she spun around and found Granger leaning against a tree with a mischievously bouncing eyebrow.

"No woman has ever referenced my odyl before. I'm sort of flattered."

"It means…"

"Animal magnetism. Yep, I know what it means. I'm just impressed you do."

"Please put on a shirt," Lydia said, averting eye contact.

"I'm hot."

"Self-aware much? I… oh shit."

"Do you always talk to woodland creatures?"

"Ugh…"

"Don't look so traumatized. It's cute."

Lydia's ovaries instantly burst into flames.

"Must be quite the cerebral rodent. You using words like strumpet and soothing anima."

"Oh my God…"

"You know, if you get tired of talking to woodland creatures…"

"How much did you hear?"

"You don't need to be embarrassed. You've been isolated for weeks. It's only natural that you would find ways to cope. When Claudia left, I found myself talking to my reflection in the mirror sometimes. Weird, right?"

"How much did you hear?"

"It doesn't matter."

"Yes it does."

"Why does it matter so much to you?"

"This is so humiliating."

"Why though? Lydia, did it ever occur to you that this weird instinct you have about me is not a one-sided thing?"

"I see what you're doing. I'm going to resist your bewitchery."

"My bewi... Lydia, why is it so hard for you to admit that we just click? It happens sometimes."

Lydia bit her lip until she tasted blood.

"In case you haven't noticed," Granger mumbled, "I've been knocking myself out trying to impress you."

Lydia blinked.

"Can I sit here with you at least?" Granger asked, cutely protruding his lower lip. "You can introduce me to your squirrel."

"Chipmunk."

"Is that spot taken?" Granger asked, pointing to a mossy patch.

"This is my office," Lydia said feebly. "It's a professional setting. It would be inappropri..."

"Is this what you're working on?" Granger asked, having already plunked his butt onto the moss and snatching some loose-leaf paper.

"Granger..."

"She drank her solitude like a potent wine," Granger read aloud.

"Granger, don't read that out loud. Jeez."

"She contemplated the water in which the fish gurgled. Like the water, she was volatile and without shape."

"I'm dead."

"This is fecking beautiful."

"It's rough."

"It's *raw*. Big difference. Do you have any more? I'd love to read whatever you've got."

"I was just..."

"Pretty damn good for someone who claims to have writer's block."

"I felt suddenly inspired."

"Really," Granger said, dimpling proudly.

"Hey, I never said that you were the reason..."

"I saved the two cans of meatball stew just in case."

"Just in case *what?*"

"I'll be at my place tonight at around 7:30," Granger said, heaving himself to his feet. "With a can opener and my irresistible odyl. If you decide to be there also, I suggest you bring your own spoon. Claudia got the cutlery in the settlement and I'm still waiting on my Amazon order."

"Granger…"

"Later, Darlin'."

CHAPTER TWENTY-FOUR

"Dammit!" Hunter swore as he threw his cell phone onto his hotel bed. From the framed artwork on the wall, the almond eyes of an expressionistic Chinese lady glared disapprovingly at Hunter from behind her feather fan.

"Ready, Hunter?" called a prematurely balding man, popping his head into Hunter's hotel room door which had been left ajar.

"In a sec, Ed," Hunter said in a muffled voice from behind his exasperated hands.

Ed eyeballed the forsaken cell phone on the quilted hotel comforter. "Calling the wife?" he guessed.

"I haven't been able to get through to her for days."

"She's fine."

"How could you possibly know that?" Hunter asked, swiveling in his chair to face Ed. "She's stranded in the woods with nobody but a deranged recluse across the lake with a morbid collection of hatchets."

"Relax," Ed smirked. "I was the same way when I first started travelling for work. I called Mary-Ella every day upon the hour, worrying she'd break her collarbone in the shower or get violated by the FedEx guy or something."

"You're not helping," Hunter complained as he gathered his laptop backpack. "I knew it was a stupid idea to buy that shack. I told her she was crazy."

"If your little woman's anything like mine, she's watching some girlie movie with a huge vat of popcorn or giving herself a home pedicure. Women are all about the self-care. It makes them feel empowered and independent. See, after a while, Mary-Ella started to get used to me not being around. Now I just get in her way. When I am there, she doesn't know what to do about it."

"I'm going to try calling again."

"We're late though."

"Dang!" Hunter said, clenching. "It keeps going directly to voicemail."

"Well there you go then! She's yapping with one of her girlfriends."

"She'd still be able to hear my call beeping in."

"Ever consider she's blowing you off?"

"Why in the world..."

"You have been kind of a dick..."

"What?"

"I heard you barking at her on the phone. I wouldn't blame her really."

"Well... she is uber-sensitive about literally everything. It wouldn't defy reason that she's holding a grudge."

"There you go then. Let's jet."

"Do you seriously think she would ignore my calls to this extent?"

"Yes. Now let's get out of here. The brunch meeting is scheduled in fifteen minutes and I want to get there before they run out of wormwood dumplings."

"But she was so needy."

"And you made it clear that her neediness was annoying," Ed said, lolling his eyeballs towards the clock. "Clearly she's adapted. Found another source of support. Talking on the phone with the parents. Girlfriends. Didn't you say she formed a weird bond with some lady who cleans toilets? Be happy for her. And move your butt before I leave without you."

Hunter filled his cheeks with air contemplatively. "You're right, Ed," he said, flinging his backpack over his shoulder. "Let's eat dumplings."

CHAPTER TWENTY-FIVE

"I brought my spoon," Lydia quavered nervously when Granger opened his cabin door. She half-playfully wagged the spoon for effect.

Granger's face glowed with rapture and perhaps relief as he evaluated Lydia approvingly. "You came," he said, almost giddy.

"I'm partial to meatballs," Lydia croaked.

"Please," Granger said invitingly, guiding Lydia inside with an outstretched hand. He seemed suddenly self-conscious of the dank room which was only partially furnished. "I set up a couple of pillows for us to sit on. By the window. I hope that's okay. Claudia took most of the furniture. She only left behind some glitchy appliances, the saggy guest cot and some odds and ends in the linen closet."

"I'm not fussy," Lydia said, obediently sitting.

Granger took a seat next to Lydia and set a steaming bowl of meatball stew in front of each of them. "The stove still works, thankfully."

"Groovy," Lydia replied stupidly.

Groovy? Oh dear God.

They chewed for an awkward amount of time.

"I should thank you," Lydia said, unable to bear the silence anymore. "For fixing my window. That was decent of you."

"Oh that," Granger said, pinkening and nervously scooping his fingers through his hair. "It seemed wrong to let you sleep in a cabin with a smashed window. Consider the mosquitos. Or I don't know…"

"The nut loaf?"

"It was the neighborly thing to do," Granger said while antagonizing a meatball with a camping spork. "Do you um… want to tell me how a cast iron skillet ended up shattering your window or would that be too forthcoming?"

"I told you, it's nothing."

"Seems kind of random to be nothing."

"You'll think I'm crazy."

"Try me."

Lydia ballooned her cheeks for a moment before blurting, "The weirdo across the lake. He came over."

Granger instantly dropped his spork.

"Did he hurt you?" Granger asked, his eyes flaring with ire.

"Not exactly, but…"

"If he did anything to you…" Granger said with his voice deepening like a protective bear.

"I'm okay, Granger."

"It's always something with that guy."

"He hasn't bothered me since you arrived."

"Do you need me to paddle over there to finish him off?"

"It was my fault, really," Lydia quavered. "I paddled over. To make friends. Then he started staring at me from his dock. Making weird phone calls..."

"How did he get your number?"

"I don't know."

"Do you lock your screen door? Is there any way he could have entered your cabin while you were out? Snooping for personal information or some such shite?"

"I never thought of that, but now that you said it, I'll never be able to unthink it."

"What did he say when he called?"

"It was mostly heavy breathing. He said he could see me. He said he could see me in my duck pajamas."

"Nefarious Creep."

"But I handled it. I... smashed my phone to smitherines," Lydia winced. "Then for good measure I hurled it into the fireplace with the charger. Impulsive, I know. But in that moment, I lost all sense of reason and went into full-on survival mode. Call it reptile brain. Think I'm loco now?"

"No. Then what happened?"

"Then for some reason he skulked around my cabin later that night. He started staring through my window, so I got scared and..."

"Oh my God..."

"So now you must think I'm a veritable lunatic. Talking to chipmunks. Feeding my cell phone to the embers. Weaponizing my cookware."

"You are not a veritable lunatic."

"So you don't think I'm losing my mind?"

"Being alone for long durations can heighten your senses," Granger said with his voice noticeably softening. "I should know. But it doesn't mean that you are losing your mind. I'm here now. I won't let you lose your mind."

"You might be slightly late for that."

"You really do need to be kinder to yourself. You are perfectly capable."

"That's not what Hunter s..."

"Who's Hunter?"

Lydia gawked with her mouth contorting into various shapes. Her heart raced at a dangerous speed as her eyes accidentally strayed and zeroed in on Granger's lips. What would have happened if she had not awoken from that dream so soon? She may never find out if she spilled the beans in that moment.

"My... ex," Lydia said, gagging on her lie.

"What did this ex of yours say?"

"He... he sometimes said that artists are unstable and delusional. But he was kidding. He said he was kidding."

"I'm not laughing."

"Ya. Neither did I."

"I think your mind is fascinating."

"One person's fascinating is another person's delirium."

"The only people for me are the mad ones," Granger said, gingerly feeling a strand of Lydia's hair between his fingers. *"the ones who are mad to live, mad to talk, mad to be saved, desirous of everything at the same time, the ones who never yawn or say a commonplace thing, but burn, burn, burn like fabulous Roman candles exploding like spiders across the stars."*

"Kerouac," Lydia whispered squeakily as Granger cupped her cheek with his hand. She closed her eyes and relished.

"Kerouac," Granger repeated, but manlier.

"Is this your way of telling me I've lost my stinking marbles?"

"It's my way of angling to see if you are as fond of Beatniks as I am."

Lydia snorted with unexpected laughter.

"I see a lot of myself in you," Granger said.

"Poor you," Lydia awkwardly attempted to joke.

"Are you going to deny that we're vibing?" Granger said, leaning in with his eyelids drooping desirously.

"Finally, I'm not the weirdest person in the room," Lydia jibed, leaning backwards the more Granger leaned in.

"You're putting up a wall," Granger said, kissing Lydia's hand.

"Nope. No wall," Lydia quibbled tremulously.

"How do you feel right now?" Granger asked, slowly slithering his arms around Lydia in an embrace.

"Safe," Lydia swallowed, feeling beads of sweat form on her forehead. "I feel freakishly safe right now. The first time in months."

"You should," Granger breathed as his lips trifled playfully with Lydia's.

"I am such a floozy," Lydia whimpered with her lips attached to Granger's.

"Shhhh, no, Darlin'. You're adorable."

As Granger's mouth meandered from her lips, down to her chin and neck, Lydia's eyes bulged with cartoonish horror when she spotted a grizzled face staring at them through the window. Her blood-curdling screams made Granger recoil and hurdle backwards.

"What the..." Granger yelped as he wiped lipstick from his mouth with the back of his hand.

"It's HIM!" Lydia shrieked, pointing at the window and cowering in the corner.

Granger turned and briefly saw the spectral face before it wafted back into the darkness.

"Son of a....!" Granger snarled as he grabbed a canoe paddle.

"Granger, what are you..."

"I'm going out there!"

"Granger, no!"

"I'm not going to let him torment you!... Us!"

"Granger, please don't! What if something happens to you? You're all I..."

Granger swerved around to face Lydia.

"... have," Lydia squeaked.

The paddle dropped helplessly from Granger's hand as he gaped dotingly at Lydia. He glanced out the window and noticed the recluse's canoe heading back across the lake, a lantern guiding the way and casting a noticeable sheen on the dark water.

"He's gone," Granger announced. "Are you okay, Lydia?" he asked, securing his hands on her forearms. "You're panting."

"What do you know about him?"

"He's just a nutter. Don't you be worrying about..."

"There's something you're not telling me," Lydia said, huddling into a ball.

"Okay," Granger exhaled. "Don't freak out or anything…"

"I hate stories that start that way."

"He… nobody learned his name… he caused some issues with the folks on the lake."

"And everybody left, blah, blah, blah. You already said that. But why did everyone leave?"

"They just couldn't take it anymore. There was something about him we all found off-putting. He intimidated everyone. With his stare. With his blatant lack of boundaries."

"What's his story though?"

"We can only guess. He literally never spoke to any of us. All we know is that he's been living on this lake for seemingly ever and he'll never leave until his days end."

"No family? No visitors?"

"Never. I lived on this lake for six years and I watched him closely. Had a wife to look out for, you know? I started noticing his behavior changing over time. Started with bouts of him talking to himself. There was a particular elm he used to have arguments with. Freaky. He had these episodes. Something would come over him. His eyes," Granger shuddered.

"So you think he descended into madness from years of isolation?"

"It's highly plausible. I can't think of any other reason for his spiral. He was only blandly weird the year I moved here, but over time… he just sort of drifted. Into some kind of morally insane headspace. The sad part is, we had a special little community here. We all took care of each other. Had potlucks. Did Filbert's runs for folks. Eventually we formed a community night watch to scope out potential… Anyhow, if the recluse had only integrated into our community, he may never have…"

"But is he dangerous?"

Granger chose his next words carefully. "It started with the Lindquists in Cabin 9. The nut loaf started stalking around their property. It was quite unnerving. Police said there was nothing they could do. But then a few people sort of… disappeared."

"What do you mean *a few people disappeared?*"

"Without a trace. Nobody could figure it out."

"You think it was him?"

"Do you have a better explanation?"

"Do you have proof even?"

"Nobody was willing to take any chances."

"What about you? Do you believe he did something nefarious? You came back here after all."

"Firstly, I didn't have a choice but to come back, seeing as how I lost nearly everything I own in that damn divorce settlement. Besides, it was mostly Claudia who wanted to board the place up for good. She never liked the lake in the first place. Too many mosquitos."

"So you're not scared?"

"He won't bother with me."

"How do you know?"

"I told you, he knows I don't take his guff."

"You keep saying that but..."

"I had a tussle with him, okay? It's not something I'm proud of, but I took him out once when there was a rumor of him gawking through my bathroom window, watching Claudia pee."

Lydia covered her mouth.

"It wasn't hard," Granger shrugged. His arms are a little floppy and well, you've seen my muscles. But still..."

"Oh my God!"

"I fractured his nose."

"Which explains why his nose is crooked."

"The witness wasn't a hundred percent sure what he saw. He was watching with his binoculars from that cottage on the rockface and he did have some significant stigmatism. But damn, it made me mad. And with all the strange happenings..."

"I... I saw a shovel wedged in a freshly upturned pile of dirt on his property that time I paddled over."

Granger gaped for a moment before replying, "Probably unrelated."

"Should... I be scared?"

"Not as long as I'm here, Darlin'."

***

"Are you sure you don't want to just stay?" Granger asked Lydia who was sitting by a crackling fire, wrapped in a thick, itchy camp blanket.

"I... can't," Lydia stumbled, feeling the scorch of a guilty heartburn.

"You can have the guest cot," Granger offered. "I can sleep on this blanket by the fireplace."

The offer was tempting. But Lydia had already breached a major wedding vow by canoodling with a non-Hunter. It was clearly a behemoth mistake to go to Granger's cottage in the first place. Patrice was a thousand percent wrong. Shameless flirting, in this case, was not harmless. Lydia's coquettishness had opened a major can or worms. A fervid, salacious and weirdly enjoyable can of worms. She could not allow the situation to become any more pleasant because she was nothing if not loyal. But damn, it was tempting.

"I gotta' go," Lydia said, standing and shedding the itchy blanket.

"Please be careful," Granger pleaded as he ushered Lydia to the door.

"He's probably in bed now. Psychopaths sleep sometimes, right?"

"Do you want me to walk you over?" Granger asked with genuine concern brewing in his eyes.

Why did he have to be so damn courteous?

Lydia squeezed her eyes shut, unable to answer.

"Tell you what," Granger offered. "How about I stand on the porch and watch you walk back. When you're inside, flick the light switch on and off so I know you made it back safely."

Lydia nodded.

"That'll be our signal from now on, okay?" Granger nodded back. "Flick the lights on and off if you're okay. Flick the lights *rapidly* on and off if you need help. Then I'll come running over."

"Sounds good," Lydia warbled.

"It would be a whole lot easier if you'd just stay though," Granger mumbled.

"I just can't, Granger. You understand, right?"

"Sure," Granger said. "There's certain things a woman's got to do for herself. I get that."

"... Right."

Before Lydia stepped outside, Granger leaned down and gave Lydia a forehead kiss that caused every nerve ending in her body to crackle with pleasure. She paused for a moment before she darted into the darkness towards her cottage. Granger craned his neck and watched intently until he saw the lights flicking on and off over at Lydia's cabin. He nodded.

"Goodnight, Darlin'," he rasped.

CHAPTER TWENTY-SIX

It took Lydia three hours to fall asleep. Her mind was whirring cyclonically, trying to analyze the events of the evening like the world's most convoluted, postmodern poem. She really should not have enjoyed Granger's company as much as she did. The delicate balance between raw attraction and a much-needed friendship was teetering on the brink of a provocative disaster. But there was something very healing about Granger's companionship. And eventually the residual coconut scent Lydia had absorbed from Granger's itchy blanket soothed her to sleep.

The soft padding of socked feet entered the dark room about and hour or so after Lydia had sunk into a deep slumber. A shadowy figure slithered under the blanket and groaned with exhaustion.

"Move over, Babe."

Lydia squirmed and grimaced in her sleep. Her eyes fluttered open when she heard the familiar whistle of Hunter's sleepy exhales.

"Hunter?" Lydia said groggily.

"Go back to sleep, Babe. Way too tired. We'll talk in the morning."

Lydia rolled over and saw Hunter's body sprawled next to her.

"What are you doing here?"

"Seriously? That's your reaction to me coming home after six months? You could at least pretend to be excited."

"I'm just so confused."

"Why? You knew I was coming home tonight."

"It can't be September already."

"Wow," Hunter yawned. "It must be true what they say about losing track of time when you're isolated in the wilderness."

"But I'm not finished my novel," Lydia said, suddenly goggling awake. "Not even close."

"Jeez, Lyds," Hunter said, rolling over to face Lydia. "You had the whole summer. What were you doing all that time?"

Lydia gaped.

"I'm... really confused."

"Why do you smell like coconut and campfire smoke?" Hunter asked, elevating himself with his elbow.

Lydia gaped.

"What's going on?" Hunter asked, suddenly accusatory. "What were you doing while I was gone?"

"Nothing," Lydia said, much too fearfully.

"Who's Jeep is parked next door?"

Lydia pulled the blanket over her head and hid.

"You didn't…" Hunter said with his eyes flaring.

"You were gone so long. Did you expect me to just…"

"Who the hell is he?"

"Nobody."

"Does he have a smoky, tropical aroma? Is that why you smell like that?"

"Hunter, you don't understand…"

"What have you done!" Hunter demanded as he clambered out of bed and stood dominantly above Lydia.

"Hunter, why are you being like this?" Lydia asked, cowering.

"After everything I've done for you!"

"Hunter…"

"I do literally everything for you while you sit at home and goof around!"

"I'm doing my job!"

"I've made all the sacrifices in this relationship so that you can do your thing, and this is the thanks I get? You go behind my back and boink Smoky McCoconut?"

"Hunter, come on!"

"I'll pound him!"

"Don't you dare!"

Lydia's face slowly melted with perplexity like a bewildered crayon in the sun as Hunter suddenly began berating her in Cantonese.

"Hunter," Lydia asked in utter confusion, "why are you berating me in Cantonese?

Hunter continued berating her in Cantonese.

"Hunter, what's going on? Why are you doing this?"

Suddenly, Hunter's violet eyes turned yellow and guinea pigs started scrambling out from under the blanket. Lydia yipped and tried to shoo them away, but the more she did so, the more guinea pigs emerged.

"Where did all these guinea pigs come from?" Lydia cried in anguish.

As Hunter began to irrationally throw balled-up socks at her in his rage, Lydia toppled out of bed and breathlessly dashed across the room to flick the light switch rapidly on and off, screaming like a banshee. Hunter snarled at her to stop it. In Cantonese.

"GRANGER!" Lydia screamed in a shrill enough octave to shatter glass.

"Who's Granger?" Hunter screamed in Cantonese.

"GRANGER! HELP!"

Within minutes, Lydia could hear a desperate pounding on the front door.

"LYDIA!" Granger hollered outside with a dramatic crack in his voice. "LET ME IN! I'M HERE! WHAT'S GOING ON!"

"If you let him in, I'll end him!" Hunter roared in Cantonese.

"I... I don't speak Cantonese so I'm just going to go ahead and let him in," Lydia sobbed.

Dodging the violently airborne socks, Lydia frantically exited the bedroom, barricading the door behind her while Hunter wailed and pounded on the door. Lydia stumbled across the dark room to let Granger in.

"Lydia," Granger said breathlessly as Lydia nearly asphyxiated him with her desperate hug.

"He's here," Lydia sobbed asthmatically.

"Who?"

"I'm so confused!"

"What's going on?" Granger said, assertively allowing himself in. "Why is the bedroom door barricaded?"

Lydia just sobbed.

Granger courageously crossed the room and removed the barricade.

"Granger! Be careful! He has socks!"

Granger scoped the empty bedroom.

"No one's here," Granger said, the bulging veins in his neck slowly subsiding.

Lydia ran to Granger and squeezed him like a juicy, Florida orange while she cried into his chest.

"I think you had a dream," Granger said soothingly, rubbing Lydia's heaving back.

"What?" Lydia snuffed.

"You're safe now, Darlin'. It's all over."

"But I saw…"

"You were sleeping."

"It was so vivid."

"I know, shhhh."

"I'm confused."

"Things will get better. We have each other now."

Lydia swallowed hard.

"Would you like me to stay?" Granger asked, wiping a tear from Lydia's face with his thumb.

"… No," Lydia nodded.

"Lydia, you're shaking. I can't just leave you here."

"It would be indecent. Maybe."

"Indecent? In what sense? We're both grownups."

"I really want you to, but… I don't know."

"What if I sleep on the couch? I'll behave. I promise."

A cringe on Lydia's face made her look as though she was in physical pain.

Why did his eyes have to be so damn caramelly?

CHAPTER TWENTY-SEVEN

Lydia awoke the next morning to the sound of a mourning dove cooing outside her bedroom window. Blinking the sleep from her eyes, she rubbed her throbbing temples and instinctively checked for guinea pigs under her blanket.

No guinea pigs.

Today would be a good day.

Rubbing her eyes with her fists, Lydia shuffled out of her bedroom and inhaled the residual scent of Granger, who appeared to have already left. His blanket was neatly folded with hotel precision and placed on the corner of the couch. Atop, was his freshly plumped pillow. Lydia noticed a copy of *Fairweather Friends Forever* sitting on the coffee table bookmarked with a Filbert's sardine coupon. Was Granger reading her book? If so, he apparently made it to chapter seven already.

Lydia's eyes widened when she found a banana muffin waiting for her on a plate, set conspicuously at the kitchen table. Alongside the muffin was an ornate display of sliced peaches, cherries and pineapple. Golden, buttered toast, cut diagonally, was featured on an adjacent plate. A champagne glass was filled with orange juice – it was one of those plastic champagne glasses meant for picnics, but still. A gingham napkin was folded into a perfect triangle, sporting a shiny fork on top.

Lydia noticed a handwritten note, folded in half and steepled next to her surprise breakfast...

"Hope you like it... Figured these must all be your favorites, seeing as how I found it all in your fridge. (Happy Face) Thanks for the couch, and don't worry. I behaved. Xoxo ... Granger."

Lydia felt herself glowing as she slid into her seat and crunched into a buttery triangle of toast.

***

When Lydia emerged from her cottage, she was alarmed to find Granger standing on top of his roof.

"Granger?"

"Hey there!" Granger waved from above.

"What are you doing?"

"The roof needs repairs. These cedar shingles have their charm, but man, they require a lot of maintenance. And they've been neglected for years so..."

Lydia winced when Granger's foot slipped on a wobbly shingle. Thankfully, he regained his footing.

"Be careful up there, okay?"

"It's all good, Darlin'! Gotta' make some headway here. There's lots to do. Still waiting on my Amazon order. They're bringing me some basic furniture and essentials."

"They may never find us out here."

"Well, there's that," Granger said, flooping the wavy locks from his forehead. "But let's hope for the best."

"Granger?"

"Ya, Darlin'? What's up?"

"Were you reading my book last night?"

"That alright?"

"Sure."

"I didn't mean to invade your privacy."

"I mean it's published, so..."

"You know, I rarely if ever read chick-lit..."

"Sorry, it's a bit girly."

"But this one's a real page-turner."

"... What?"

"I would have finished it in one sitting, but I nodded off at around 4:00 a.m."

"Understandable."

"If you don't mind, I'd love to..."

Lydia gasped when she saw Granger's foot smash right through the roof. Losing his footing, he toppled gracelessly from the roof and landed with a cringeworthy thud on the ground.

"GRANGER!"

Lydia frantically ran towards Granger, who was lying on a carpet of cedar needles with his leg splayed angularly. He yowled with agony.

"Granger, oh my God!"

"Dammit!"

"Is it broken?"

"Hell if I know!"

"Can you move it?"

Lydia winced at the painful warble Granger uttered while trying to move his leg.

"What do I do, Granger?" Lydia said, caressing the sweaty hair across his forehead. "Tell me what to do."

"Drive me to the hospital? My Jeep keys are…"

"I can't drive," Lydia blinked.

"At all?"

Lydia shook her head apologetically.

"Call an ambulance then. Please. My cell in in my jeans pocket."

183 - Lovesick Lake

"You want me to..."

Granger howled in pain.

"Okay," Lydia said, flapping her hands around like an overwhelmed chicken. "I'll just..."

Lydia slid her little hand into Granger's back pocket, flushing like a nincompoop. Yes, his butt was every bit as firm and unyielding as she had imagined. Quickly removing the phone, her fingers trembled as she prepared to dial.

"What's the number of the closest hospital?"

"St. Dymphna Medical Centre. Check my contacts."

Fumbling pathetically with the phone, Lydia eventually found the number.

"I'm on hold," Lydia quavered with the cell phone to her ear.

"Dammit."

"What kind of an inept hospital puts a person on hold?"

"Not sure if they send ambulances out here..."

"Why? How far is it?"

"Twelve hours."

"The closest hospital is twelve hours away?... Frig! The battery's drained. Where's your charger?"

"Ah shite."

"Oh for the luvva... you have no charger?"

"It's in my Amazon order…"

"What are we going to do now?"

"Have you ever set a bone?"

"Are you serious right now?"

"I'll talk you through it."

"Are you even qualified?"

"Basically…"

"Granger…"

"Do you see a bone sticking out?"

"I don't think so," Lydia said, squishing her eyes shut and looking away.

"Drag me into my cottage. I think I've got everything you need there."

"I feel sick."

"You'll do fine, Darlin'."

An involuntary grimace consumed Lydia's face as she hooked her arms underneath Granger's torso. She had fantasized about groping his chest from the moment she first laid eyes on him, but this was not exactly the way she envisioned it. Granger mewled like an injured moose when Lydia yanked his body backwards towards his cottage, leaving a grooved trail in the sandy dirt.

"I've got you," Lydia said, grunting from exertion.

"I know you do," Granger winced.

CHAPTER TWENTY-EIGHT

"So I just did that," Lydia said, wrenching from the duress of having literally just set a broken leg. A statuesque, athletic leg. Attached to a delectable snog muffin. Despite her sobbing and involuntary quivering throughout the entire process, Lydia managed to follow Granger's instructions commendably by splinting his leg with a broken canoe paddle and tightly tied pillowcases. She had pulled the guest cot in front of the fireplace in the main living area and tucked Granger in with his injured leg elevated.

"Thank God you were here," Granger shuddered in a cold sweat.

"Hopefully I didn't screw up your leg too badly," Lydia said as she placed a cold, wet facecloth on Granger's forehead. "Do you need anything?"

"Do you have any pain killers?" Granger winced.

"Of course I have pain killers, I'm a writer."

"I'll take one. Or ten."

"I have some at my cottage."

"Please don't go."

"How else can I..."

"Can you stay? Please?"

"I should ride my bike to Filbert's and see if I can use the phone to call the hospital."

"Go tomorrow."

"But you're shivering. You might have an infection."

Granger clutched Lydia's arm tightly as his eyes glossed up at her pleadingly.

"...Okay," Lydia swallowed.

"Tonight? Can you... can you stay tonight?"

"Tonight?" Lydia asked, already feeling guilt constrict her throat.

Granger nodded earnestly.

"Granger, I... I don't think I can."

"I don't want to be here alone."

"I can check on you whenever..."

"Lydia..." Granger said with a crack in his voice that made Lydia's conscience scream.

"I'll... I'll at least need to grab a few things from my place..."

"Thank you."

"And you have to promise you'll let me ask for the phone at Filbert's tomorrow. I have no idea what I'm doing here and if you die or your leg falls off, that's on *me*, Granger."

"Understood."

"Okay, here I go," Lydia said, now sweating more profusely than Granger. "I'm about to dash across the way to my cottage. To get stuff. For... tonight."

"Please hurry?"

***

Wobbling from trepidation, Lydia began frantically shoving arbitrary things into a black, garbage bag: a toothbrush, her pillow and a threadbare quilt, three towels of varying sizes, a fistful of panties, raisins, a mosquito coil, a kitchen sponge, a can of creamed corn, a Leonard Cohen nightshirt, antiperspirant, one sock, cheese, a deck of cards and a vial of patchouli essential oil. (Thanks, Patrice)

Lydia scoured her cabinets for her stash of Tylenol 3's which she had stockpiled before her move to ensure she had enough for her periodic migraines. She scarfed about three bottles from the shelf, tossing them into the garbage bag. While she was at it, she grabbed some vitamin C and a prescription bottle of expired muscle relaxants.

Before she darted back to Granger's cottage, she noticed her copy of *Fairweather Friends Forever* sitting hopefully on the coffee table, right where Granger had left it with the ridiculous sardine bookmark. Lydia stuffed the book in the bag.

***

Dragging the bulky garbage bag into Granger's cottage with an unladylike grunt, Lydia became aware of an odd silence in the air. Granger was unmoving on his cot next to the crackling fire.

"Granger?" Lydia quavered.

Lydia studied Granger's face which was as pale and lifeless as a glob of plasticine. "Granger?" she said with a worried staccato, pulling his eyelids open with her thumbs. "Are you dead?"

Granger's lips pursed in an attempt to quell laughter. "If you're trying to kill me, you're going to have to try harder," he rasped feebly.

"I brought some Tylenol 3's," Lydia said, trying to breach the childproof seal with nervously tremoring hands. "How many do you…"

Lydia swore when the pills scrabbled all over the floor. She scrambled to rescue every single one while creeping around on her hands and knees.

"I am so daft," Lydia whimpered while lunging for a rogue pill that was about to roll under the refrigerator.

"Don't say that, Darlin'."

"I'm doing everything wrong."

"Come here," Granger urged.

Still trembling, Lydia cherry-picked two pills from the floor that appeared to be relatively uncontaminated and offered them to Granger. He popped the pills into his mouth with an open palm and gulped before chasing them down with a swig of water.

"You are a rockstar," Granger said fondly as he wiped some water from his upper lip.

"Hardly."

"Can you imagine how this would have played out if you hadn't moved in next door?"

"In such a scenario I wouldn't have distracted you while you were on the roof."

"So now you're blaming yourself for being beautiful and interesting?"

Lydia instantly paled like an anemic parsnip. She blinked way too many times while grappling for her garbage bag. "Need anything else? Creamed corn? Patchouli? A fistful of... oh dear God..."

"Why are you so nervous?"

Lydia squeaked.

"Please tell me you're not afraid of me," Granger said with a twinge of sincerity in his voice.

Lydia shook her head fervently.

"Then why are you fumbling around like a traumatized baby giraffe?"

"I'm not afraid of you, Granger. I'm... afraid of... me."

Granger's lips parted.

"I really shouldn't be here," Lydia quavered.

"I'm glad you are."

"I know I just..."

"Sit near me?"

"Granger, there's something you don't know about me..."

"I know everything that matters."

"And yet you don't."

"What else did you bring in that bag?"

"Can you please let me finish my thought process? I need to tell you something and I'm not sure how..."

"Darlin', I'm in a lot of pain right now and you've doped me up pretty good with these pain killers. This might not be the best time to tell me something important."

"Fair enough," Lydia blinked.

"Do I see a book peeping out of that bag?" Granger asked hopefully.

"I... I thought since you started reading it last night that you might..."

"Can you read it to me?"

"Like out loud?"

"I'm feeling kind of foggy…"

"I've never really…"

"It's just us."

"I mean the reason I write is so that I can express myself without actually having to…"

"Please?" Granger asked, batting his eyelashes cutely.

Feeling the blood rush to her face, Lydia nodded, took the book and sat cross-legged on the floor next to Granger's cot with the fire sputtering sparks behind her in the fireplace. She swallowed hard as Granger wriggled with anticipation under his blanket. Cracking open the book and trying to regulate her shallow breaths, Lydia began to stutter the beginnings of Chapter Seven.

"She… she walked alone in the throng. Solitary as a mollusk, clamped tightly in her shell. Yet surrounded by legions of carbon-based lifeforms. Her friends were there but weren't. For Catherine's brand of friendship appealed to those who crave friends but have no interest in being a friend back. Still, she went through the motions for the sake of conformity. Conformity, after all would protect her from herself. The only thing that made sense to Catherine was… Mildew."

Granger groaned contentedly.

"This sounded a whole lot better before I said it out loud," Lydia grimaced.

"Your voice sounds like a little song sparrow," Granger lulled hazily.

"Nobody even says that," Lydia giggled ironically.

"You are correct. But I am a mite high right now."

"Already?"

"Oh true apothecary, thy drugs are quick…"

"See? You're loopy. I could sound like an aviary of screechy pterodactyls and you'd still think I sound pretty reading this."

"Keep going, please."

"Really?"

"Listening to you read is like the most righteous, spiritual experience. Pretty much ever."

"You're fun when you're high."

Granger playfully kissed the air in Lydia's general direction.

Lydia's constricted chest gradually slackened, making it a little easier to breathe as she turned the page.

"Mildew, as usual, was admiring his collection of garden gnomes…"

***

Was it creepy for Lydia to stare at Granger while he was sleeping? Probably. But there was no chance of her ever falling asleep on her makeshift bed composed of a row of pillows on the hard floor with a tired quilt strewn on top. She set up her temporary bed next to Granger's cot so she could be literally right there if he needed anything after they had nestled in for the night.

Sadly, sleeping on a pillowed floor is not as comfortable as it sounds. Compounded by the fact that Lydia was worried sick about Granger. She felt responsible for his freak accident and dreaded the idea of him slipping into a coma or having his leg rot off because of her rookie medical malpractice.

He stopped shivering, which was a good sign. His forehead felt cool when she placed her hand on it. Only his left cheek was pinkish and that was due to its proximity to the fireplace. At last, his fever had broken which reduced Lydia's checklist of worries by one item. She dabbed a dribble of blissful sleep-drool from the corner of his mouth with the damp facecloth she had once used as a cold compress.

"Of course, you're teddy bearishly cute when you're sleeping," Lydia whispered. "Just when I thought you ran out of reasons for me to succumb... You are an incredibly dangerous influence on me, Granger.... Or maybe a dangerously incredible influence..."

"NOOOOO!" Granger yelped, suddenly writhing around in his sleep.

"Granger?"

"Gourds!" Granger moaned. "With faces on them!"

"Granger, wake up."

"Get them away from m…" Granger said so loudly that he woke himself up. "What… where… I… Lydia…"

"Are you okay?"

"I think I just had a trippy fever dream."

"That's impossible, given that your fever broke a couple hours ago," Lydia said, squeezing Granger's hand. "It's more likely a codeine trip."

"That'll do it," Granger said, catching his breath and ogling Lydia's nighttime garb. "I'm really digging your Leonard Cohen nightshirt."

"Oh… thanks," Lydia said, trying to make herself comfortable on her stupid pillows. "Try to go back to sleep."

"How are you even comfortable down there?"

"I'm fine."

"I think maybe you should crawl in here with me," Granger said, patting the spot in the cot next to him.

Ominous silence.

"Lydia?"

"Yeah, no, that's not a possibility."

"There's no point in you waking up with a stiff back tomorrow."

"Just no, okay?"

"Do I really have to admit that I'm afraid to go back to sleep after that bizarre dream I just had regarding root vegetables?"

"Nice try."

"I'm being serious here. You're not the only one who gets weirdly surreal dreams."

"... Okay," Lydia said, resigned as she scootched into the cot next to Granger where she laid stiff like a plank next to him.

"I've never slept with a girl with a Leonard Cohen nightshirt before. It's kind of hot."

"We're not *sleeping together.* At least not in the Biblical sense."

"And all it took was for me to break my leg," Granger winked.

"That's kind of a drastic way to get a girl in bed."

"Kind of makes me wish I had broken my leg days ago."

"Behave."

"There's not much I can do in the way of misconduct with a fractured leg."

"Well, there's that."

Awkward pause.

"So..." Granger tried, "is your novel autobiographical?"

"Of course not," Lydia shifted uncomfortably.

"Not even a little bit?"

"Why is it that everyone thinks writers only write about themselves? Sometimes things are just fiction."

"You seemed so sympathetic to Catherine's plight."

"I'm a sympathetic gal. Plus it's my job to make people care about my characters."

"Wow, that's something," Granger marveled. "The way you just tuned in to Catherine's mind like that. You really grasped how she felt when those three twats exploited her friendship for personal gain, then ditched her when she needed them the most. I cried a little."

"I don't base any of my characters on real people," Lydia said, genuinely believing what she was saying. "My three friends are nothing like Mercedes, Denise and Julia."

"You only have three friends?"

"No," Lydia snuffed sarcastically. "There's also Eliza."

"So you're sure that a little smidgeon of yourself never seeps into your characters? Even subconsciously?"

"My characters are merely figments. Always. Archetypes of societal flaws. In general."

"Interesting. It's just that your work is so introspective, so I was just wondering."

"Introspective. That's exactly what Hunter complained about…" Lydia said, abruptly stopping.

"So he wasn't good to you?" Granger asked, turning his head to face Lydia's on the pillow next to him.

"What? I mean, yes. Yes, of course he is... was good to me."

"Then why aren't you together right now?"

"He... went to Shanghai," Lydia said, not exactly lying.

"You didn't want to go with him?"

"I've told you how I feel about large cities."

"So Gunter..."

"Hunter."

"... chose to end his relationship with you instead of..."

"I don't think it's fair to talk about Hunter when he's not here to defend himself."

"Sorry," Granger apologized. "I mean, I'm freshly single myself so I guess failed relationships are kind of on the brain right now."

"I didn't fail. Are you saying you think it's my fault?"

"What I mean to say is..."

"Because if you are saying it's my fault then you would be correct."

"What do you mean?"

"Hunter had nothing to do with... it."

"He chose to leave."

"I let him go."

"He didn't have to go."

"Can we just not? This is a whole lot more complicated than what you are assuming."

"If it makes you feel any better, Claudia shagged her psychotherapist, Dr. Fluggendorfer."

"Why would that even make me feel better?"

"Dr. Lola Fluggendorfer."

"Dude! That's unfortunate."

"It is what it is," Granger shrugged. "Now she's Lola's problem."

"You seem to be taking this in stride."

"It was hard, being suddenly turfed to the curb with little to no worldly possessions. But you know what was harder? Being constantly gaslit by the world's swankiest succubus. On the bright side, she had handsome bone structure in her face, and she enjoyed Scrabble. But I'm not going to miss the mood swings."

"I can't believe she did that to you though. With someone named Lola Fluggendorfer."

"I claim responsibility for my part of it. I was the one who suggested she needed psychotherapy. And I stand by that suggestion."

"That must have stung."

"Not as much as it stung when she made out with the divorce lawyer in the elevator. With me standing literally right there."

"How did you put up with her for..."

"Nine years."

"Nine years?"

"We married when I was nineteen and unworldly. Naïve might be a good word to describe it. I invested everything into that girl but didn't get much back, you know? Kind of like Catherine in your book. Except, well. I'm much more ruggedly virile than Catherine," Granger winked.

"But you're so optimistic," Lydia said, inadvertently snuggling closer to Granger. "So smiley and good-natured. I had no idea you'd been through so much."

"A huge weight was lifted from my shoulders that I didn't even realize was there. Besides, if the timing hadn't worked out the way it did, I wouldn't currently be snuggling next to a refreshingly cute, creative genius. And Leonard Cohen, in an indirect way."

Lydia's eyeballs twitched with humility.

"Nor would you be suffering a hairline fracture in your fibula," Lydia smirked ironically.

"Well, there's that."

CHAPTER TWENTY-NINE

"I'm not asking you to bootleg aphrodisiacs into a Catholic finishing school for virgins," Lydia said exasperatedly to an emotionless, squinting version of Henrik the following morning. "I just want to use the damn phone."

Henrik squinted even more scrutinizingly.

"It's an emergency," Lydia continued. "My friend broke his leg and neither of us have a functioning cell phone with which to call the hospital. He hasn't even had an X-ray or anything. I had to set it myself using a broken canoe paddle. That's not something that I generally do!"

Henrik narrowed his eyes with more stubbornness.

"Why are you still staring at me like that? Do you even care that Granger is in severe pain? Like, towel-biting, *'I-think-I-just-saw-Jesus'* pain! Look, I really don't know what I'm doing, and we need a doctor or an ambulance. I'd even settle for a veterinarian or a versatile orthodontist. I'm literally begging you!"

Henrik folded his arms challengingly.

"Oh, I see," Lydia nodded sardonically. "You want me to buy something first, is that it? Fine, I'll play. I'll take this here can of aerosol spray cheese. Then can I use the phone? Or do I have to throw in a bag of ranch Doritos and a Styrofoam cup of dew worms?"

Henrik gave off some kind of nuance that summoned a few, equally unnerving locals with similar staring problems. They just sort of emerged from behind various shelves and a Pepsi cooler, each giving Lydia a penetrating stare. One of them guarded the only visible phone in the room by using himself as a human shield.

"Elsewherians are weird," Lydia seethed.

***

"What is wrong with the people in this village?" Lydia blustered as she burst into Granger's cottage. "Here, have some aerosol spray cheese."

"I'm guessing they didn't let you use the phone at Filbert's," Granger said as he hauled himself into a sitting position in his cot.

"Henrik the Eyebrow just stared at me like the headlights of an alien spacecraft," Lydia complained. "I'm telling you, the locals here are devoid of empathy. How could they refuse me a phone when you so obviously need help?"

"I'm going to be okay," Granger said, inviting Lydia into a hug. "You did a smashing job on this splint. And these pills you brought over are making this a lot easier."

"You need a doctor."

"It'll heal by itself with time."

"What if you need surgery?"

"I don't think it's that bad. Probably just a hairline fracture, like you said."

"We won't even know that until you get an X-ray."

"You can try again at Filbert's tomorrow."

Lydia stiffened with dread.

"Or we could wait until my Amazon order arrives. Then I can charge my phone..."

"Granger, you can't even plunk the coordinates of this place into a GPS. There's a very good chance the Amazon drivers will never find us."

"Then I'll wait a few more weeks and then drive myself to the hospital."

"Don't you dare."

"Lydia, would you just relax?" Granger said, kissing Lydia's forehead. "You are giving me everything I need."

"I'm such a dolt. What kind of a grown-ass woman doesn't know how to drive?"

"You've lived in the city all your life. What reason would you have to drive with public transit at your fingertips? Please, let's just sit here and enjoy some spray cheese."

Granger offered Lydia the aerosol can and gestured for her to spray cheese into his mouth. She complied and did likewise.

"How did you sleep?" Granger said, attempting to change the subject.

"Fine," Lydia said, still pouting, her mouth still full of the questionable cheese.

"Sorry my furniture hasn't arrived yet," Granger said, humbly running his fingers through his hair. "I had intentions of making things a bit more comfortable. For me. For guests. And stuff."

"I really didn't mind the cot," Lydia said, accidentally blushing.

"I guess I won't be doing much refurbishing with this bum leg. Maybe..."

Lydia swerved her head around to face Granger.

"I don't know," Granger said awkwardly. "I was just thinking that maybe what this cottage needs is a... woman's touch."

"As in me?"

"Claudia did all the decorating. Which is why she felt entitled to literally everything in the settlement, I guess. I think I'm a little over my head here. I don't have much experience in this kind of thing."

"Neither do I," Lydia admitted. "My apartment in Toronto was shabby chic but not on purpose. And minus the chic. Because poverty. And when I moved into Cabin 6 the place came furnished."

"Doesn't mean you don't have a kind of female flair."

"What does that even mean?"

"You have your own sense of style."

"Perhaps you failed to notice that I shop in thrift stores."

"It works."

"So you want me to, what? Fix up your cottage with a keen eye for that enviable *Starving-Writer-Funky-Funk* motif?"

"If you're up for it," Granger said with a coy dimple.

***

"If I'm up for it?" Lydia vented to Rocky in the privacy of her writing alcove. "He wants me to help him fix up his cottage, Rocky. Me. Because apparently, I have some kind of elusive *woman's touch* and I don't even know what that means. Is this weird? This is weird, isn't it. I mean fixing up some guy's cottage and being asked to put my own personal thumb print on the thing is kind of an intimate request. I barely know the guy!"

Chitter, chuck, chuck, chuck.

"That's not fair, Rocky," Lydia answered the chipmunk ironically. "I HAD to sleep over at his place. In his cot. He was in pain. Because of me, no less. I couldn't just... Okay, I could have said no. It was just hard to refuse because Granger is so... much in pain. Dammit, Rocky! I've officially cheated, haven't I. Just slap a big old scarlet letter on my forehead right now."

Rocky cocked his head.

"See, if I don't help the guy out with his cottage, how will he make the place livable for himself when he'll be incapacitated for six to eight weeks? I'm not a bad person for wanting to help out a neighbor who has literally nobody else, right? I mean, I would do this for him even if he didn't have intriguing hair. And eyes that make my insides wobble. And a physique that resembles a Greek statue. And that fetching patois that melds together both unpretentious, rural jabber and lofty, literary diction. That's a rare quality, by the way. Shows that he's educated without being a snob. My favorite combination of two things. But I'm doing this for the sake of community. My pleasure endorphins have nothing to do with this."

Chit, chit, chuck.

"That's a valid point, Rocky," Lydia answered ironically. "What constitutes cheating, really? I mean, Hunter is essentially cheating on me with his job. If you think about it, the way Hunter has been treating me lately could be considered spousal neglect. He's not honoring our wedding vows. So how is it fair that I'm over here, clutching my fidelity like a miserly woman with her pearls? Waiting like a Labrador retriever for Hunter to come home while he's out there having an actual life? Let's keep it real. Hunter is in love with industrial plastic."

Rocky was nonplussed.

"So yeah," Lydia nodded, trying to convince herself. "I'm not in the wrong here. I deserve to be happy too. Yeah. So there's that. So... why is this so hard?"

Rocky startled and darted away when he heard a clambering noise echoing from across the lake. Shielding her eyes from the sun, Lydia squinted at the recluse who appeared to be in the process of burying a large, bulky object. Lydia's eyes bulged with fear and morbid curiosity. When the recluse turned his head in

Lydia's direction, he glared across the lake, slowly raised his arm and pointed ominously at Lydia.

With a gasp of horror, Lydia ducked down in her alcove, behind her rocky refuge.

"Why won't he just leave me alone?" Lydia whimpered to herself.

CHAPTER THIRTY

"A loud, clambering noise?" Granger asked as Lydia brought him a tuna fish sandwich on a paper plate.

"How did you not hear it?" Lydia asked, sitting on the cot next to Granger with a sandwich of her own. "The sound amplified across the lake like a clangy death metal guitar in a concert stadium. I don't even want to guess what he was burying."

"And he pointed at you?"

"What was up with that?"

"It's beyond weird."

"You… believe me, right?"

"Of course, I believe you."

"You don't think I'm hearing things. Seeing things."

"If you say the nut loaf pointed at you for reasons that only make sense to him, then I one thousand percent believe you, Darlin'."

"But you didn't hear the clambering noise."

"That doesn't mean it didn't happen. I'm doped up on codeine, remember?"

"Codeine makes you not hear things?"

"Anything can happen when your brain is fluffy... What's this?" Granger asked, picking up a dainty, little flower from atop his sandwich and examining it curiously.

"It's an edible flower," Lydia explained. "I plant them in my garden patch."

"Well look at you, being all self-sufficient," Granger gleamed proudly. "So do you eat it or is it just for decoration?"

"They are surprisingly delicious," Lydia beamed. "I know I'm not supposed to, but sometimes I can't resist plucking a few for a snack. I bring a little dish over to my writing alcove. Go ahead. Try."

Granger gingerly tasted the flower and his face ignited with surprise and delight. "Wow."

"Right?"

"Are there more of these? I could get used to eating flowers."

"I've got a whole patch full of them. I never knew how much I could enjoy salad before I started growing these little beauties," Lydia said, feeding her own edible flower to Granger.

"What's in the boxes?" Granger asked, jerking his head towards some boxes Lydia had dragged over from her cottage.

"I found some things in my cellar that I thought might make your cottage a little, I don't know, homey."

Granger craned his neck expectantly.

"Tell me if you hate any of this, okay?" Lydia said, rummaging through a box. "I found a welcome mat with a loon on it. To make people feel welcome."

"Love me a good loon."

"A vintage lamp," Lydia continued. "You'll probably have to put it on the floor until you get more furniture, but it is what it is. I could plausibly bike over to Filbert's and ask the Eyebrow if he could order me some furniture, but I would prefer not to subject myself to that. So maybe we should go for an eclectic, kind of retro style?"

"I'm down with that."

"Sweet. I did find a patio dining set. It's just the cheap, plastic kind with faux Adirondack chairs, but if I give you the checkered tablecloth from my kitchen table, it should be cute enough. I can pick some flowers and put them in a little mason jar, so it feels more like a dinner table. Oh! I also found these classic snowshoes. I thought you could hang them crisscross over the fireplace. It'll make the room feel all woodsy. Here's some gently used tea candles, a fun shag rug, buffalo check curtains, inspirational fridge magnets, and artificial fern... Do you like ottomans? Because I found an ottoman."

"You are so cute when you get like this."

"Like what?"

Granger shrugged mischievously.

"...Okay then... I couldn't find any artwork in the cellar, and these walls could use some cheering up. How would you feel if I painted the artwork? Like myself?"

"You paint?"

"Well, not officially... ever. But I would love to try. I mean, how different can it be from writing? I'm just telling a story with paint."

"Do you have paint?"

"Oh... I hadn't thought of that."

"Can you use house paint? I think I have some in my shed, left over from when I started painting the cottage. We kind of left in a hurry so I didn't finish."

"Huh. I was actually wondering why only half of your cottage was painted... Sure, I can use exterior paint. There's no rules when you have no clue what you're doing. Speaking of which, do you like lasagna? I thought I'd try making one and bringing it over this evening. I think I have almost all of the ingredients."

"Well look at you, being all domesticated."

"Lasagna or no lasagna?" Lydia said, shooing away the awkwardness in the air.

"I never turn down a good meal," Granger winked.

"You're quite confident it's going to be edible."

CHAPTER THIRTY-ONE

Lydia teetered across the room, carrying a pan of lasagna with her oven-mitted hands. She placed it on the plastic, patio dining set which she had configured by the window, adorned with her own checkered tablecloth. As promised, she put a single, flirty daisy in a water-filled mason jar and positioned it in the middle of the table.

"I didn't have any cottage cheese or tomato sauce," Lydia apologized as she peeled the aluminum foil off the pan," so I had to make some substitutions." She tilted her head critically as she evaluated her virgin lasagna. "Is the top supposed to be black like that?"

"I can't wait to dig in," Granger said with an encouraging wink.

"Should I bring you over a slab of this thing?" Lydia asked cot-ridden Granger.

"After you went to all the trouble of composing a full-on bistro table by the window?" Granger teased. "Heck, no. I want to go on a date with the cutest girl on Lovesick Lake."

"Funny," Lydia said dryly.

"How about you drag me over?"

"Won't that be a little cumbersome with your botched leg…"

"Come on, Girl. You should be old hat at this by now."

"But you're safe over there with your leg elevated in a splint... what if I break you?"

"Already broken, Darlin'."

Lydia groaned as she shuffled hopelessly towards Granger's cot. Squinting and sucking the side of her cheek contemplatively, she tried to formulate in her mind how it was geometrically possible to move Granger to the table, factoring in their size difference, the fragility of his sloppily splinted leg, the laws of gravity and the various ways she could optimize her minimal, upper body strength. After mentally crossing herself, (which was weird, seeing as how she was not Catholic) Lydia wrapped her arms around his chest, which was both nerve-throttling and weirdly titillating.

"Pretend like you're hugging me," Lydia grunted with her face muffled in his chest.

"Like this?"

"Not there, more around my ribcage."

"Are you sure about that?"

"Don't ask questions, I have a plan."

"Ow, my leg..."

"Can you just kind of angle..."

"I don't think you can bend that way."

"Hold on, I'm going to try something else."

"That didn't work."

"Let me try..."

"Why are your arms doing that?"

"Grunt."

"Are you sure this is..."

"Would you just..."

FLUMP!

After a failed attempt at heaving Granger upwards and contorting her body unnecessarily, Lydia accidentally bellyflopped on top of Granger, finding herself oddly splayed atop his body. She groaned from embarrassment, although, Granger could not stop laughing.

"Awkward," Lydia grunted.

"Is it though?"

"Don't be cheeky," Lydia said, trying to wriggle free.

"Moi?"

"Why aren't you letting go?"

"You told me to pretend I'm hugging you."

"Granger..."

"Am I doing a convincing job?"

"You're high."

"A little bit."

Lydia was doing a noticeably half-ass job at squirming inside Granger's hug. She stopped entirely when she met Granger's eyes which were glassy from desire and codeine. They stared stupidly at each other for an awkward amount of time while a screaming match took place between Lydia's conscience and id. Her id presented a convincing argument.

"Crap," Lydia winced.

Granger raised an inquisitive eyebrow.

"Now I have to snog you."

Before Granger could respond, Lydia urgently pulled the blanket over their heads. Then two, shapeless blobs undulated suggestively underneath.

"So much nope," Lydia said consensually from under the blanket. Her voice sounded like it was smooshed against another pair of lips.

Then suddenly...

BOOM!

"Did you hear that?" Lydia asked, instantly stiffening.

"What?" Granger said dreamily, while nibbling Lydia's ear.

"That noise."

"I didn't hear anything."

"Didn't you feel the earth move?"

"Is that a line?" Granger giggled. "That's lame."

"Granger, seriously. There was a loud boom and the cabin rattled. Like a little earthquake or something."

"Are you okay, Darlin'?"

"This is the second time I've heard a loud, conspicuous noise that you seem to be completely oblivious of. Please tell me you're not messing with my head..."

"You know I would never..."

"I couldn't have been the only one who heard that."

"Lydia..."

"Please tell me you heard that noise."

"But I didn't..."

"Granger, please."

"It's possible that with you being alone here all this time... I mean, they say that isolation can make you hear things..."

"Please."

"I won't lie to you, Darlin'," Granger said gingerly. "I can't tell you I heard something when I didn't."

"What's happening to me?"

"You're going to be okay," Granger promised. "Some people can't acclimate to isolation, is all. But I'm here now..."

"This is embarrassing."

"It's really okay."

"I'm supposed to be a self-reliant woman," Lydia said, shedding the blanket, sitting up and curling herself into a ball. "I shouldn't be so dependent on other people. That's pathetic."

"It's human."

"You don't understand…"

"Tell me then."

"I have to prove…"

"What do you have to prove? And who to?"

"Hunter didn't think I could handle this on my own. He doesn't think I'm good at adulting."

"But…"

"He talks down to me all the time," Lydia sniffled. "Even the nickname he gave me implies that I'm naïve and helpless."

"But…"

"And now I've proven him right. I've been on my own, what? Like thirty-seven seconds and now I'm completely falling apart. Hearing things. Having loopy dreams. Sabotaging my cell phone in a state of debilitating panic…"

"But…"

"Everything he said about artists… about *me* is true. I'm just… I don't know. Fragile."

"But…"

"Hunter…"

"... is not here. He's not here anymore, Lydia. Why does his opinion of you even matter now?"

Bulging with fear, Lydia's eyes wondered across the room. Granger squinted questioningly.

"What..." Granger began. "... what are you..."

"The window," Lydia said with a whispery squeak, somewhat like a mouse that was about to be chewed on by a sadistic cat.

Granger suddenly swerved around when he heard relentless banging on the window. The recluse was outside, pounding on the glass and yelling something that was garbled and unintelligible.

"Ah shite!" Granger snarled, impulsively jolting out of bed. Then remembering his broken leg, he yowled in agony and crumpled to the floor.

"What are we going to do?" Lydia cried, wincing with each bang on the window.

"Where did he go?" Granger asked, nursing his throbbing leg. "I don't see him at the window anymore."

Both Lydia and Granger jolted when they heard the recluse banging on the door, demanding to be let in.

"Board up the windows!" Granger boomed.

"What? I..."

"Hurry, Lydia! I can't move! My leg!"

After blinking a few times from shock, Lydia fumbled around the room, collecting the planks of wood that were piled near the fireplace.

"Hammer!" Granger yelled, pointing at his toolbox. "Nails!"

"Ugh!" Lydia stammered. "Hammer and nails. Got it."

With tremoring hands, Lydia breathlessly hammered the wooden planks to every window while Granger barked orders at her to barricade the door. Lydia dragged a wooden chest in front of the door while the recluse pounded harder and howled louder and more insanely.

"Leave us alone!" Lydia screamed.

Lydia shrieked as a hatchet blade sliced through the door.

"GRANGER!" Lydia screamed.

"Get the paddle!" Granger yelled, trying to drag himself towards the canoe paddle that was leaning against the wall. Clutching it in his hand, Granger slid the canoe paddle across the floor, towards Lydia.

"What do you want me to do with this thing?" Lydia sobbed.

"The fire!" Granger screamed while pointing at the fireplace.

"You want me to..."

"Hurry!"

Trembling, Lydia dipped the paddle into the fire, igniting it. Then with a desperate battle cry, she hurled the flaming paddle through the window. A dark shadow outside cowered, dodging away from the paddle and scurrying towards the waterfront. Lydia breathlessly watched the recluse as he toppled urgently into his canoe and disappeared into the night. Lydia tried to announce that the recluse was gone but she was hyperventilating.

"Lydia, are you okay?" Granger asked, catching his own breath.

"He... He..."

"He's gone," Granger finished for her. "We put the fear in him. Might think twice about coming back for a while. Safety in numbers I guess, right?"

Lydia nodded but was too scared and out of breath to reply verbally.

"Come here," Granger coaxed.

Lydia crumpled into Granger's embrace and sobbed."

"Shhhh," Granger soothed. "He's gone.

CHAPTER THIRTY-TWO

"Industrial plastic is the stuff progress is made of," Hunter said into a reverberating microphone to scads of international professionals. He licked his lips when nobody in the crowd grasped his attempt at ironic humor. "The name's Hunter Knapp. I represent *Crudderson's Textiles,* established 1933, in case any of you are taking notes. Some of you may be asking yourselves, *'why industrial plastic?'* Why not industrial foam? Rubber? Composite material? Sheet metal? Or perhaps some nice rayon? Friends and colleagues, I am eager to share with you today my enthusiasm for industrial plastic. I'm really excited about it, actually and by the end of my talk, I am sure that you will absolutely fall in love with Lydia."

The blank silence that hung in the air for an embarrassing amount of time basically punched Hunter in the face with realization. He paled and gaped at the perplexed faces staring back at him. Ed washed the humiliation from his face with a swipe of his hand on Hunter's behalf.

Nervously rummaging through some loose-leaf paper at his podium, Hunter ironed over his incredibly awkward error.

"Plastic," Hunter said quickly to quell the din of confused murmurings in the crowd. "Of the industrial variety. That is my passion. My life. I dream it. Breathe it. Drink it. Metaphorically. Please don't try to drink it. I admire industrial plastic for a plethora of reasons. Would you like me to list them?"

From his seat, Ed squinted at Hunter in a WTF kind of way.

"Robust," Hunter continued. "Dependable. Unyielding. Versatile. Waterproof. Still can't relate to my zeal? You will. Oh, you will. Let me tell you about how Crudderson's sets ourselves apart from the other, more pedestrian, dare I say *vanilla* industrial plastics. Ours has been tested by some of the deftest physicists in the world. For example, Lydia Northrop... *Leonard Northrop,* PhD. My apologies. I seem to be off my game today... Uh..."

Ed gave Hunter an inquisitive look as Hunter just shrugged back at him.

"Crudderson's industrial plastic is revolutionary because it cannot be penetrated, lacerated, cracked, set on fire or left entirely alone for six months..." Hunter winced, then recovered. "Because one product is not nearly enough. You'll want a whole collection of them. They're just that good. Now some of you may be concerned about the effect industrial plastic has on, and I use air quotes, *the environment.* Perhaps you are uneasy about the fact that our product can never truly biodegrade due to its indestructible constancy. I used to always get an earful from Lydia..."

Ed slapped his forehead.

"The point I'm trying really hard to make," Hunter recovered, "is that the environment will forgive you because when you use a product that lasts, you don't need to replace it time and time again. Hence, less waste. How strong is our industrial plastic? Let's just say that not even a hatchet..." Hunter suddenly stopped, paled and stared blankly at something indecipherable in the air for three solid seconds. "Excuse me," Hunter said, suddenly leaping from the stage, hurrying sideways through a narrow row of chairs towards the door at the back of the conference room.

"Hunter?" Ed called as he followed him into the lobby.

When Ed found Hunter, he was on his cell phone, standing next to an ornate fountain.

"What the heck happened in there?" Ed chirped.

"I'm on the phone."

"You're going to ruin this for us. Did you even hear yourself just now?"

"Lydia's still not answering."

"Why are you still trying to get through to her? She's never going to take your calls at this point. Can't you take a hint?"

"I'm going to call the police."

"Why?"

"So they can check up on her."

"Are you effing serious? You've clearly already pissed her off and now you're sending the fuzz to spy on her?"

"I'm just taking care of her."

"Did it occur to you that she might not want you to take care of her? Think about it, she's blowing you off, clearly because you're condescending..."

"Condescending?"

"You talk about that woman like she's in junior high school. If my wife heard me talking about her that way, she'd thump me."

"So she's punishing me, is that what you're saying?"

"And if she's punishing you for being condescending, imagine the ire you would stoke if she knew you were having her supervised in your absence. Do you want a divorce? Because I'm pretty sure that's grounds for divorce."

"So… she's punishing me. For being condescending."

"And for deserting her, but that's none of my business."

"So you don't think anything's wrong."

"Dude, she's floating around on a raft right now, developing skin damage. That's just about all that's wrong. Now, you have to go back in there and salvage that conference or we are all screwed."

"I don't know if I'm up for it."

"Be up for it or we're all out of a job!"

Hunter bit his lip.

CHAPTER THIRTY-THREE
(SIX WEEKS LATER)

Lydia awoke in the morning to the sound of a page turning. Rolling over she smiled up at Granger who was sitting contentedly in bed, reading *Fairweather Friends Forever.* She welled with a sense of pleasureful calm, secure in her bed with someone who felt like a twin flame. She could not remember the last time she felt cozy in her bunny hug of uniqueness. She could say her name without wincing from self-doubt. Over the past six weeks, her breathing patterns slowly started becoming more natural and she was starting to lose her stutter.

But that niggling feeling, like a remorseful cherry pit embedded in her conscience, reminded her that she was basically a tart.

She did not deserve Granger, her conscience kept nagging her. He was basically everything she ever wanted. Authentic. Literary. Empathetic. Intuitive. Everything she did not even know she needed. But Hunter would eventually return and then what would happen to Grydia? (The celebrity couple name Lydia conjured in her imagination) While her conscience barked at her to end things now before anything became more perfect, Lydia yearned for at least a little more time to absorb this weird and wonderful thing that was happening between herself and Granger.

But an even larger cherry pit of remorse was gnawing at Lydia's conscience, more obstructive and invasive than the first. She tried her best to suppress it as this moment was just too perfect.

"And done," Granger said, closing the book satisfactorily.

"And it only took you six weeks to finish reading it."

"I didn't want it to end," Granger shrugged. "Just wanted to savor everything."

Lydia knew the feeling.

"I think I'll be able to drive to the hospital for an X-ray today," Granger said, massaging his leg which was no longer in the splint."

"Are you sure?"

"I'm doing much better. I barely need the walking stick anymore."

"I would hate for you to aggravate it."

"You fixed me," Granger said, lovingly straightening Lydia's bedhead. "I couldn't have gotten through this without you."

"I'm coming with you."

"Sure thing. Just let me pee and then we'll jet."

Lydia ambled out of bed, stretched and pulled on a vintage smock dress. She hastily combed her hair with her fingers, smelled her armpits and slipped her feet into some flipflops. Moments later she turned to find Granger standing in the bedroom doorway with a look of ashen marvel glazed to his face.

"Granger?"

"I... I found this in the bathroom."

Pinkening, Lydia swiped a pregnancy test from Granger's hand.

"I peed on that thing so you probably shouldn't..."

"Why didn't you tell me?"

"I was going to grab a couple more of these from Filbert's to make sure..."

"Am I... am I the..."

"The stick says two weeks and you're literally the only one around so..."

"Oh, Darlin'!" Granger said reverently, cupping Lydia's face with his hands.

"I mean I got the test from Filbert's so it's probably a sketchy brand. Who knows if it's accurate?"

"Oh my God!" Granger said giddily. "Oh my GOD!"

"So you're okay with this?"

"I am absolutely over the moon!"

"We should really talk about..."

"I've always wanted... Claudia thought babies were reviling. She thought they had weird heads. So we never..."

"Granger, there's a fairly large issue we need to..."

"I am on such a high, I don't think anything could bring me down right now!"

"Never mind then," Lydia swallowed. "Maybe we should just go to the hospital?"

"I'll go on my own. You stay here."

"Why?"

"It's a bumpy drive. I don't want to disturb the embryo. What if he shakes loose or something?"

"I don't think…"

"You take care of yourself," Granger said, hobbling towards the door with his walking stick.

"Granger, we really need to talk."

"I'll be back before you know it. We'll have all the time in the world to talk then."

"Granger…"

"Love you, Darlin's."

"What's with the plural… oh."

Lydia watched through the window as Granger hobbled towards his Jeep. He revved the engine excitedly, spun the wheels in the dirt for effect and howled with glee as he sped down the driveway. Lydia swallowed hard.

***

"Things got out of control very quickly," Lydia confessed to Rocky while crouched in her writing alcove. "How could I have let this happen? I mean, in my defense there's slim pickings when it comes to buying birth control in the boondocks when the only retail outlet is a sketchy general store, manned by an antisocial rube. That's the last time I use contraceptives in the form of strawberry chewables."

Squeee, squeee, squeee, chitter chuck.

"How is this going to work, even?" Lydia asked the chipmunk, tossing her hands in the air. "Hunter will be home in September. Oh my God. I won't be able to hide this from him by then. Or hide Hunter from Granger. Or Granger from Hunter. Maybe I should just hide."

Chit, chit, chit, chuck, chuck.

"How am I supposed to know?" Lydia answered Rocky ironically. "I don't even know how I feel about all of this. Granger and I became very close, *very* quickly. I'm not sure I want to give that up. Not yet anyway. And maybe this embryo is a sign... But I made a promise to Hunter. I'm in love with him too, right? I think so anyway. It's hard to compare when Hunter isn't here as a frame of reference. Everything is just so damn confusing."

Rocky cocked his head.

"Agreed," Lydia nodded. "I have the embryo to think about now. He needs his daddy. And it's doubtful that Hunter will willingly assume the role. Unless I can somehow convince Hunter that the embryo is his. But he's not stupid. And that wouldn't be fair to Granger. He's so excited. This is hard. No offence, Rocky but things would be a lot less overwhelming if my only source of counsel wasn't a chipmunk."

The sound of tires crackling over the gravel caused Rocky to scurry away skittishly. Lydia discovered a police cruiser slowing to a halt in her driveway. Inside the car was a pair of officers who appeared to be consulting an address. Lydia secured the paper she had been writing on under a rock and approached the police cruiser inquisitively.

"Officers?" Lydia croaked when one of the officers emerged from the vehicle.

"Morning," the officer said with a humble salute. "Just checking in here. Are you Lydia?"

Lydia nodded uncertainly.

"Are you okay?" the officer asked.

"In what sense?" Lydia asked suspiciously.

"We were sent over to see how things are going."

"Is this a typical service around here or…"

"I don't have permission to divulge details," the officer apologized.

Lydia blinked.

"You're alive," the officer observed, writing something down.

"Last time I checked."

"And you don't seem to have any injuries."

Lydia shook her head.

"That individual across the lake? Has he been bothering you?"

"Why? Was there an incident or..."

"Just asking."

"He was stalking and trespassing, and he made some inappropriate phone calls..."

"Hmm."

"He hasn't been around in weeks. But maybe you could investigate him anyway. He's weird."

"Any reason why you haven't been answering your phone?" the officer asked, still writing.

"How did you..."

"Someone, who's name I cannot disclose is wondering why you haven't been taken his calls for the past six plus weeks."

Lydia's lips parted.

"Everything okay?" the officer asked, lolling his eyeballs from his notepad.

"I don't have a phone... anymore."

"Oh... Listen, I shouldn't be saying this, but would you like to use my phone to call your husband?"

Lydia instantly stiffened and her eyes bulged with anxiety.

The officer's facial muscles relaxed in a state of realization and empathy. "I see," he said softly, crossing something out on his notepad. "Nobody can make you do something you don't feel comfortable doing."

"I mean..."

"That's okay," the officer said, putting a reassuring hand on Lydia's shoulder. "You know your boundaries and that's okay."

"It's not like that! I'm just not ready..."

"None of my business," the officer said, waving from the cruiser as they pulled out of the driveway. "I'll let him know everything is fine."

Lydia gaped.

CHAPTER THIRTY-FOUR

"Don't you think it's a bit early to be thinking about names?" Lydia asked.

Granger paddled the canoe to the center of the lake, where the setting sun sprayed a shimmeringly orange beam across the water. He stopped paddling in such a place that it seemed like they were being illuminated by a Broadway spotlight. Not only was Granger on cloud nine about the embryo, but the x-rays he obtained at the hospital the day prior indicated that his leg was nearly healed and would not require surgery. Granger wanted to celebrate by warming up a frozen pizza to share in the canoe. Although Lydia was feeling woozy for a variety of reasons.

"Do you like Tennyson?"

"You know I do."

"Not the poet. The name."

"For a baby?"

"Why not?"

"I… yes. Yes, I do actually," Lydia mumbled.

"I was also thinking maybe Hemmingway, Marlowe, Stoker, Hugo, Ovid…"

"And if it's a girl?"

"Bronte, obviously," Granger chuckled.

"Obviously," Lydia murmured.

"You don't seem to be as into this as me," Granger observed. "Are you feeling okay?"

"I really need to talk about something."

"Okay."

"But I don't want to."

"Then don't."

"But you really need to know about this, Granger. I can't keep this from you anymore. It's wrecking me."

"Are you rethinking the notion of us using a literary name? Because we could go with something more conventional if..."

Granger was interrupted when Lydia spotted a police car in the distance, pulling into her driveway.

"This again," Lydia sighed.

"What are the police doing at your place?"

Lydia waved at the police from the canoe, hollering across the lake that she was still fine. After waving back, the police departed.

"What do you mean by *still fine?*" Granger asked.

"They were here yesterday when you were at the hospital. Checking up on me."

"Why?"

Lydia pursed her lips for what seemed like forever.

"Lydia?"

"Hunter."

"What?"

"Hunter sent the cops."

"Why?"

"To keep an eye on me."

"What?"

"I know."

"That's twisted. Is he still trying to control you somehow or…"

"It's complicated."

"Is he obsessed with you?"

"Granger…"

"I'm just trying to understand here, seeing as how the two of you aren't married anymore…"

"We… are."

"You are what?"

"… Married."

"To Hunter?"

Lydia nodded guiltily.

"So the divorce isn't finalized?"

"We're not..."

"You're not divorced?" Granger asked, looking ashen.

"I wanted to tell you... but didn't want to tell you."

Granger gaped.

"Granger, I am so sorry. I didn't mean to meet you. I didn't mean for me to get so attached to you."

"I'm trying to process..."

"Are you mad? Because I feel like you should be mad."

"Just give me a minute!" Granger said unintentionally loudly, while squeezing his eyes shut and waving his hands around frantically. "Everything in the world that matters to me was an illusion and I can't wrap my brain around it, can you understand that?"

Lydia nodded submissively.

They floated aimlessly in the canoe for an undetermined amount of time.

"What do we do?" Lydia finally asked.

"I suppose that ball is in your court now, isn't it."

"I need you to tell me what to do."

"You made a commitment to Hunter."

"So... when he comes home in September..."

"What about little Tennyson?"

"Technically, he's just genetic material at the moment."

"Pretty soon he'll have a face and then shit will get real."

"Maybe I should just…" Lydia stuttered. "I mean, I'm not ready to let you go. And the way I see it, things won't be the same anymore between Hunter and I."

"So you think things will be the same between us now?"

Lydia swallowed hard.

"You've kept this from me for a long time," Granger droned.

"I know."

"Is this why you were so tentative at first?"

"I was confused. I've never felt this close to someone before."

"I wish you had told me."

"Me too."

"But if you had told me earlier then we wouldn't have…" Granger's eyeballs lolled up and down Lydia's body.

"Maybe…" Lydia tried. "… Maybe we should just go for it."

"Really?"

"Why not? I've already fudged everything up. Why not do what feels good?"

"What about Hunter?"

"We have until September to figure that out."

CHAPTER THIRTY-FIVE

"Can't it wait until September?" Ed practically squeaked as Hunter hurled some arbitrary articles of clothing into his suitcase.

"I have to take care of something at home," Hunter said without breaking his stride.

"Lydia is not in crisis," Ed groaned. "She's doing fine without you. Why is it so hard for you to understand that she's not helpless without you? Give her some credit, man!"

"You don't understand."

"Come on! Stop being like this! We have to go over this presentation for tomorrow! Everything is riding on this!"

"You're on your own, Ed."

"Are you nuts?"

"I'm getting a flight out tonight. Something's wrong."

"Something's wr... Hunter, you sent the cops and they said she's holding up great. Without you."

"I'm going."

"Hunter, how is this going to look? Crudderson's is ruthless! They'll replace you in a heartbeat if you bail like this! Everything you've ever worked for will disappear in a puff of purple smoke!"

"It's not open for discussion," Hunter said, rolling his carryon luggage out of the room.

"You'll never get another opportunity like this one!" Ed beseeched. "You'll lose everything. How can you pay down your property in Elsewhere if both you and Lydia are unemployed?"

"I hate this shitty job anyway," Hunter said with dead eyes. "Besides, I left something at home."

"What?"

"Everything."

CHAPTER THIRTY-SIX

The recluse stood on his dock, squinting in consternation at Lydia, who in the distance, was scribbling madly in her notebook in what should have been the privacy of her rocky alcove. Somehow, he appeared more foreboding than usual with grave thoughts creasing his forehead. His eyes remained glued on Lydia, focusing on her every move.

Rubber tires on gravel made the recluse's ears twitch. Shortly after, the sound of a minivan door sliding open and children's voices calling for their grandpa made the recluse turn his head. His face suddenly warmed into a grandfatherly smile as little ones ran uninhibited into his open arms. He knelt down to their level, enjoying the ambush of hugs and kisses.

"Grandpa!" bubbled little Tommy.

"Take it easy!" the recluse laughed heartily. "I'm going to drown in kisses here!"

"Good to see you, Dad," Z.J said, giving the recluse a familiar pat on the back.

"How was Europe?" the recluse asked.

"It was cool!" little Sally piped up. "We saw French things and the *Awful Tower!*"

"That's not what it's called, Dummy," Tommy jibed.

"I'm sure it was plenty awful," the recluse said, giving Sally a doting squeeze. "I wish I could have seen it with you. If it wasn't for this nasty bout of arthritis…"

"Zeke!" came a voice that made the recluse's jowls quiver with emotion.

"Don't you ever leave me again," Zeke said, pulling his dear wife in for an urgent embrace, "you hear?"

"Just wasn't the same without you, Zeke," Ruby said, wiping a tear from her husband's cheek. "Did you mind your arthritis? Your pills?"

"I'm fine, Ruby," Zeke said fondly. "Just glad my whole tribe is back with me again. This bachelor life is for the birds."

"Did you eat well?" Ruby persisted.

"Beans, mostly."

"Oh, Zeke," Ruby said, flapping Zeke's shoulder with the back of her hand. "You at least used a fork, didn't you?"

Zeke looked sheepish.

"What am I going to do with you," Ruby chuckled.

"Never eaten alone in more than fifty-five years," Zeke shrugged. "Who else did I have to impress?"

"I'm making rump roast tonight," Ruby announced. "With utensils. The first decent meal you've had in six months."

"No arguments here."

"How did you manage, Dad?" Z.J. asked, putting a hand on his dad's shoulder. "A whole six months on your own. Did your joints give you any trouble?"

"Things were good, mostly," Zeke inhaled. "Only one thing's been troubling me though."

"What's that?"

"A strange girl moved in across the lake there. I think there might be something wrong with her."

"Really? What do you mean by strange?"

Zeke craned his neck, watching Lydia venture into her cottage.

"Come along and I'll show you."

***

"I think she might have moved here from the city," Zeke explained while Z.J. paddled the canoe across the lake towards Lydia's property. "I could tell she wasn't accustomed to the rustic life. The husband hasn't been around for a while and the friends seem to have stopped coming. I reckon she got a mite lonely."

"So why do you think something's wrong with her?" Z.J. asked.

"After a while," Zeke explained, "she started acting, I don't know. Off. Sneaking around my place. Flailing her arms. Screaming. She got paranoid. Had these fits. Flicking the cabin lights on and off. I came by a few times to check up on her, but she went wild. I think living alone out here might have made her snap."

"Poor girl," Z.J. said.

Once they landed the canoe into the shore, Zeke took his son to Lydia's writing alcove.

"She calls it Rocky," Zeke said, pointing to a small river rock with peanut shells scattered around it. "And she talks to it."

"Oh my God," Z.J. said, ashen.

"And over there," Zeke added, pointing, "there's a little patch of dirt that she tends compulsively."

"A garden?"

"No, Son. Dirt. There's nothing there to tend. I don't think she knows there's nothing there."

"Jeez."

"And more concerning still, I often see her eat flowers. She just plucks them from the ground and shoves them into her mouth like a snack. I've never seen anything like it."

Zeke and Z.J. ducked for cover when they spotted Lydia walking towards Granger's cabin with a large, plastic bowl of potato chips.

"There she is," Zeke stage whispered.

***

"I brought chips," Lydia said hopefully.

Granger half-smiled.

"Salt and Malt," Lydia coaxed. "Your absolute favorite."

"You do know me better than anyone," Granger mumbled.

"Are you ever going to trust me again?" Lydia pouted.

"I've never been *the other man* before."

"That's not how I think of you, Granger."

"You realize that this is exactly what Claudia did to me."

"I... know."

"Do you know how that made me feel?"

Lydia shrugged hopelessly.

"I feel sick at the thought of me putting someone else through what I did," Granger grunted.

"Because you are a decent person," Lydia said, straddling Granger in his chair. "Please, Granger. Let me prove to you that I'm a decent person too. I need you."

"Lydia..."

"I like myself more when you're around," Lydia pleaded. "Because of you, I'm the best possible version of myself. If you give up on me, I'll lose myself. Again."

"You bring out the best in me too," Granger admitted while twiddling with a strand of Lydia's hair.

"It'll be awkward," Lydia said. "Because I always make things awkward. But I know I can figure it out as long as I can feel..."

"My soothing anima?" Granger smirked.

Lydia threw her head back and laughed explosively.

**

"One day she just started pulling the boards off the windows," Zeke explained to his son as they discreetly peered through Granger's window. "She started coming over here every day with food. Dragging furniture over. One time she got me so worried I came over to see if she was okay and she threw a flaming canoe paddle at me, right through the window."

"Did you call the police?"

"Sure did. Told them to swing by and check things out."

"And?"

"The police said she seemed fine. She was out in the canoe and waved to them like a normal person."

"What in the world is on the walls?" Z.J. asked in bewilderment as he caught a glimpse through Granger's window.

"Who the heck knows?" Zeke shrugged. "I suppose she think's it's art. She broke into the neighboring shed, snatched some buckets of exterior paint and just… went at it."

"Wait," Z.J. said, shielding his hands over his eyes as he peered through the window. "Is there someone in there with her?"

"Let me see," Zeke said, squinting through the window alongside his son. "Well, I'll be! She's talking to someone. I didn't think anyone was there, but this would explain why she's been bringing over food and such."

"Who do you think it is?"

"Could be one of them squatters again. Maybe someone claimed the place and she's been helping him out?"

"That could be dangerous through," Z.J. pointed out. "The squatters we've come across have often been unstable and territorial. Not to be mean, but she looks a little… I don't know. Wholesome. Naïve maybe. If that guy's a squatter in there, he could easily take advantage."

"Don't I know it."

"We should do something."

"She'll wig out if we…"

"Dad, we can't just leave her alone in there with a criminal."

Zeke blew the air out of his cheeks. "Here we go again then."

***

Lydia savored the flavor of Granger's lips. He had clearly borrowed her boysenberry Chapstick. Her eyes fluttered open when she heard something shuffling outside the window.

"Wait," Lydia hesitated. "Someone's out there."

"Not again," Granger groaned.

Lydia leaped from the chair and flattened her body against the wall next to the window, craning her neck to get a glimpse of the intruder. "Oh God," she cracked. "There's two of them now."

"Dammit."

"Granger, we have to run."

"Where the heck..."

"We'll take your Jeep!"

"Are you crazy? I'm not going out there. And neither are you!"

"We can't just be sitting ducks.."

"It's the feckin' recluse though!"

"Granger, come ON!"

"Lydia, DON'T!"

CHAPTER THIRTY-SEVEN

Groggy from jetlag, Hunter stumbled into the cottage, where he found the screen door unlocked.

"Lydia?" he called into the empty, hollow room.

Something was different.

Everything was different.

For one thing, half of the furniture was missing and the smashed, kitchen window was pathetically sealed with zigzagged masking tape. With growing concern, Hunter ravaged the cottage in search of Lydia or any sign of what had happened to Lydia. He found her smashed cell phone in the fireplace, mangled from the heat and poking out of the ashes.

Hunter's heart raced.

"Lydia!" he screamed.

The bedroom was empty, but the blankets on the bed were twisted and thrashed around as though there had been a struggle.

In the kitchen, save for the window, everything seemed to be normal except for the fact that the cutlery drawer was missing.

The moment Hunter entered the bathroom, he winced from a strong ammonia smell. He found a dozen or so popsicle sticks strewn all over the bathroom counter and floor. There were pee stains on every single one.

"Oh my God. LYDIA!"

***

When Hunter began to scour Lydia's writing alcove, he found some paper she had pinned beneath a rock.

"Her new novel?" Hunter quavered to himself.

Reluctantly he read, but the handwriting was nearly indecipherable. He squinted, trying to interpret.

"Granger dripped with enigma and murky water," Hunter read frantically, but not aloud. His eyeballs quivered as he read each line. *"Guinea pigs and socks. Guinea pigs and socks. Where did all these guinea pigs come from? And just like the lake, bottomless with ideas, there he stood like a burning planet. Caramel. Triangles. Kerouac. In that moment, my eyes became two lemurs, ready to pounce with abandon. He came from inside. Eat the flowers, Granger. Flowers and burnt lasagna are all I have but at least I didn't take the whippets. I would never take the whippets, for you are my triangle. Shhh. I won't tell. Tennyson was composed of strawberry chewables but that wasn't my fault. Can I emerge with you, out of the black water like the undulating otter? He came from inside. The chipmunk is the sacred, transcendent oracle of the abyss and will not abandon me like the others. Others. Others. The eyebrow is watching. Inside. If you wish to*

drown, do not torture yourself with shallow water. Granger. They call me Granger. But you can call me the caramel god. The albatross."

"What the hell is this?" Hunter squeaked with horror.

CHAPTER THIRTY-EIGHT

Lydia was not entirely sure why she climbed the tree, but it seemed like a good idea at the time. She lost track of Granger in the kerfuffle, being pursued by the recluse and whoever the hell else that other guy was. Hence, the tree seemed like a safe enough bet. The recluse did not seem spry enough to climb trees. The other guy she was not as sure about.

Up in the tree, Lydia clutched the boughs tightly, straddling over a thick branch. Her breath tremored as the recluse and his minion stood at the base of the trunk, looking up imploringly at her.

"Come on down and let's talk, Honey," Zeke begged.

"Get away from me!" Lydia screeched.

"It's going to be okay," Zeke promised. "Z.J. and I just want to help, is all."

"Granger!" Lydia shrieked like a velociraptor.

"What's going on here?" Hunter demanded, jogging and panting towards the tree.

"Hunter!" Lydia screamed. "Oh, thank God!"

"Sir," Zeke said, extending a trembling hand for Hunter to shake, "I'm Zeke from across the lake. Is this…"

"My wife," Hunter panted desperately.

"Where's Granger?" Lydia cried.

"Who's Granger?" Hunter asked.

"GRANGER!"

"Who are you talking about, Lydia?" Hunter asked, while holding up her novel manuscript. "And what the hell did you write? It's like the ravings of a madwoman. And why did you pee on all those popsicle sticks?"

"You have to help me, Hunter!" Lydia sobbed. "The recluse…"

"The who?" Zeke asked.

"He's been stalking me!"

"I was just trying to help, Sweetheart. I didn't mean to scare you."

"You called me relentlessly…"

"How would I even get your number?"

"Hunter, listen to me," Lydia cried breathlessly. "Find Granger! He knows the lake! He knows what to do!" Lydia spotted Granger ambling towards the tree. "Over there! That's him!"

Hunter, Zeke and Z.J. all turned their heads.

"Granger!" Lydia screamed, nearly falling from the tree while waving for him. "GRANGER! Over here!"

"Lydia?" Hunter's voice cracked.

254 - Allison McWood

"Hunter, please," Lydia beseeched. "I know it's obviously going to be awkward between you and Granger. But you need to work together. Trust each other. The recluse…"

"Why does she keep saying that?" Zeke asked, scratching his head.

"Hunter," Lydia swallowed, "I'm sorry about what happened between me and Granger. And I hope you can love our baby like a special uncle or something…"

"Lydia…"

"Why isn't anyone apprehending the recluse?" Lydia freaked. "Granger? Granger, why are you just standing there? Do something!"

"Lydia," Hunter said with tears streaming down his face, "there's no one there."

Sweating profusely, Lydia turned to Granger who suddenly dematerialized into a flurry of ethereal particles, then faded into nothingness.

A series of images rapidly flashed through Lydia's mind…

FLASH: Granger is thumping his heel against his rotting dock, saying to Lydia that the dock is *barely able to support the two of them* and that *it's a wonder they don't both go crashing right through.*

FLASH: At Filbert's General Store, locals stare as Lydia is talking, flirting and locking eyes with seemingly nobody.

FLASH: Henrik gives Lydia a strange look when she is purchasing men's underwear. She refers to a man who is not there.

FLASH: Granger and Lydia share the quote, *"...solitude can quickly destroy reason."*

FLASH: Granger lustfully quotes Kerouac. *"The only people for me are the mad ones."*

FLASH: Granger tells Lydia that he sees a lot of himself in her.

Realization suddenly struck Lydia that Granger was not standing in the spot she had once seen him only moments ago.

Lydia fainted.

In the depths of her own mind, Lydia could hear her own voice echoing in the darkness...

"They call me mad, while they are all mad themselves... Plautus."

A WORD FROM ALLISON:

My readers begged me for a quarantine book, so here you go.

Ever wonder what happens to a writer's mind when forced into isolation for months at a time? (Insert sadistic giggle) Since the entire world has collectively lost its mind during the Covid 19 lockdowns, I thought I'd be festive and write about the effects of isolation on the human mind. Fun, right?

You might notice that *Lovesick Lake* is a little darker than my other books. But you should still be proud of me because I somehow managed to warp it into a comedy. So if your mind is a bent as mine, you will still laugh your butt off, despite the theme being uncharacteristically serious. And since every single one of you, (minus a few of you in Sweden) has been denied social interaction for the past year, hopefully you will relate to this weird, little book.

The setting of *Lovesick Lake* is completely fictional and there is no relationship to the RV camping resort of the same name in the Kawarthas. (Although if you're into that kind of thing, I hear that resort has great reviews)

ACKNOWLEDGMENTS

Big thanks to Charis Orchard for first believing in this story and encouraging me to write from my heart. I want to give you a hug once hugs have been decriminalized.

Thanks also to Lindsay Weening-Brown for your astute grammatical observations and Professor Derek Cohen for teaching me how to convert darkness into comedy. And a shout-out to Marie Laporte for driving to the remote outskirts of freaking nowhere to find me some inspirational lake water.

Special thanks to Dan for existing, Tammy for helping me stay ridiculous throughout a dark year, Brian May for his uplifting Instagram posts, the AFM community for making the pandemic a little less pandemic-y, my canoe for being a conduit of happiness, my childhood imaginary friend who believed in me as much as I believed in him and that random chipmunk in Algonquin park. (You know who you are)

Pardon My French

A Romantic Farce

Written By **Allison McWood**

LOGGED IN
A Laugh Out Loud Romantic Comedy!

Allison McWood

Allison McWood is an acclaimed, multi-published Canadian author, playwright and lyricist. Specializing in comedy, farce and satire, Allison's novels, plays, musicals and children's books all feature her signature quirkiness. Her writing has not only charmed readers and audiences across Canada, but her works have also been taught at Universities around the world from Vancouver to Lucknow, India. Holding a specialized Literature/Renaissance Drama degree from Toronto's York University, Allison is also a Shakespearean dramaturge, and Marlovian scholar.

When she is not writing, you can either find Allison in her red canoe, reading way too many books, playing air guitar, petting all the dogs or sipping cappuccino in a cute cafe.

www.instagram.com/annelidpress/